Joyce
Marx
Hardy
Defoe
Abbott
Melville
Machiavelli
Montaigne
Chesterton
Cooper
Emerson
Austen
Hugo
Eliot
Grimm
Haggard
Stoker
Carroll
Christie
Molière
Wilde
Byron
Maupassant
Schiller
Engels
Garnett
Einstein
Fitzgerald
Hawthorne
Smith
Kafka
Goethe
Dostoyevsky
Hall
Cotton
Kipling
Doyle
Willis
Baum
Henry
Nietzsche
Leslie
Dumas
Flaubert
Turgenev
Balzac
Stockton
Vatsyayana
Crane
Burroughs
Verne
Whitman
Gogol
Vinci
Curtis
Tocqueville
Busch
Homer
Widger
Tolstoy
Darwin
Thoreau
Twain
Scott
Plato
Potter
Freud
Zola
Lawrence
Dickens
Harte
Kant
Jowett
Stevenson
Burton
Hesse
Andersen
London
Descartes
Cervantes
Poe
Aristotle
Wells
Voltaire
Hale
James
Hastings
Cooke
Bunner
Shakespeare
Richter
Chambers
Irving
Doré
Dante
Chekhov
Shaw
Wodehouse
Benedict
Alcott
Swift
da
Pushkin
Newton

tredition®

tredition was established in 2006 by Sandra Latusseck and Soenke Schulz. Based in Hamburg, Germany, tredition offers publishing solutions to authors and publishing houses, combined with world-wide distribution of printed and digital book content. tredition is uniquely positioned to enable authors and publishing houses to create books on their own terms and without conventional manu-facturing risks.

For more information please visit: www.tredition.com

TREDITION CLASSICS

This book is part of the TREDITION CLASSICS series. The creators of this series are united by passion for literature and driven by the intention of making all public domain books available in printed format again - worldwide. Most TREDITION CLASSICS titles have been out of print and off the bookstore shelves for decades. At tredition we believe that a great book never goes out of style and that its value is eternal. Several mostly non-profit literature projects provide content to tredition. To support their good work, tredition donates a portion of the proceeds from each sold copy. As a reader of a TREDITION CLASSICS book, you support our mission to save many of the amazing works of world literature from oblivion. See all available books at www.tredition.com.

 Project Gutenberg

The content for this book has been graciously provided by Project Gutenberg. Project Gutenberg is a non-profit organization founded by Michael Hart in 1971 at the University of Illinois. The mission of Project Gutenberg is simple: To encourage the creation and distribution of eBooks. Project Gutenberg is the first and largest collection of public domain eBooks.

Montaigne and Shakspere

J. M. (John Mackinnon) Robertson

Imprint

This book is part of TREDITION CLASSICS

Author: J. M. (John Mackinnon) Robertson
Cover design: Buchgut, Berlin – Germany

Publisher: tredition GmbH, Hamburg - Germany
ISBN: 978-3-8472-1534-9

www.tredition.com
www.tredition.de

MONTAIGNE AND SHAKSPERE

BY

JOHN M. ROBERTSON

LONDON
THE UNIVERSITY PRESS, LIMITED
16, JOHN STREET, BEDFORD ROW, W.C.
1897

THE UNIVERSITY PRESS

1

MONTAIGNE AND SHAKSPERE

For a good many years past the anatomic study of Shakspere, of which a revival seems now on foot, has been somewhat out of fashion, as compared with its vogue in the palmy days of the New Shakspere Society in England, and the years of the battle between the iconoclasts and the worshippers in Germany. When Mr. Fleay and Mr. Spedding were hard at work on the metrical tests; when Mr. Spedding was subtly undoing the chronological psychology of Dr. Furnivall; when the latter student was on his part undoing in quite another style some of the judgments of Mr. Swinburne; and when Mr. Halliwell-Phillipps was with natural wrath calling on Mr. Browning, as President of the Society, to keep Dr. Furnivall in order, we (then) younger onlookers felt that literary history was verily being made. Our sensations, it seemed, might be as those of our elders had 2 been over Mr. Collier's emendated folio, and the tragical end thereof. Then came a period of lull in things Shaksperean, partly to be accounted for by the protrusion of the Browning Society and kindred undertakings. It seemed as if once more men had come to the attitude of 1850, when Mr. Phillipps had written: "An opinion has been gaining ground, and has been encouraged by writers whose judgment is entitled to respectful consideration, that almost if not all the commentary on the works of Shakspere of a necessary and desirable kind has already been given to the world." 1 And, indeed, so much need was there for time to digest the new criticism that it may be doubted whether among the general cultured public the process is even now accomplished.

To this literary phase in particular, and to our occupation with other studies in general, may be attributed the opportunity which still exists for the discussion of one of the most interesting of all problems concerning Shakspere. Mr. Browning, Mr. Meredith, Ibsen, Tolstoi—a host of peculiarly modern problem-makers 3 have been exorcising our not inexhaustible taste for the problematic, so that there was no very violent excitement over even the series of new "Keys" to the sonnets which came forth in the lull of the analysis of the plays; and yet, even with all the problems of modernity in view, it seems as if it must be rather by accident of oversight than for lack of interest in new developments of Shakspere-study that so little attention has been given among us to a question which, once raised, has a very peculiar literary and psychological attraction of its own—the subject, namely, of the influence which the plays show their author to have undergone from the Essays of Montaigne.

As to the bare fact of the influence, there can be little question. That Shakspere in one scene in the Tempest versifies a passage from the prose of Florio's translation of Montaigne's chapter Of the Cannibals has been recognised by all the commentators since Capell (1767), who detected the transcript from a reading of the French only, not having compared the translation. The first thought of students was to connect the passage with Ben Johnson's allusion 4 in Volpone 2 to frequent "stealings from Montaigne" by contemporary writers; and though Volpone dates from 1605, and the Tempest from 1610-1613, there has been no systematic attempt to apply the clue chronologically. Still, it has been recognised or surmised by a series of writers that the influence of the essayist on the dramatist went further than the passage in question. John Sterling, writing on Montaigne in 1838 (when Sir Frederick Madden's pamphlet on the autograph of Shakspere in a copy of Florio had called special attention to the Essays), remarked that "on the whole, the celebrated soliloquy in Hamlet presents a more characteristic and expressive resemblance to much of Montaigne's writings than any other portion of the plays of the great dramatist which we at present remember"; and further threw out the germ of a thesis which has since been disastrously developed, to the effect that "the Prince of Denmark is very nearly a Montaigne, lifted to a higher eminence, and agitated by 5 more striking circumstances and a severer destiny, and altogether a somewhat more passionate structure of man." 3 In 1846, again, Philar敗 Chasles, an acute and original critic, citing the passage in the Tempest, went on to declare that "once on the track of the studies and tastes of Shakspere, we find Montaigne at every corner, in Hamlet, in Othello, in Coriolanus. Even the composite style of Shakspere, so animated, so vivid, so new, so incisive, so coloured, so hardy, offers a multitude of striking analogies to the admirable and free manner of Montaigne." 4 The suggestion as to the "To be or not to be" soliloquy has been taken up by some critics, but rejected by others; and the propositions of M. Chasles, so far as I am aware, have never been supported by evidence. Nevertheless, the general fact of a frequent reproduction or manipulation of Montaigne's ideas in some of Shakspere's later plays has, I think, since been established.

Twelve years ago I incidentally cited, in an essay on the composition of Hamlet, some dozen 6 of the Essays of Montaigne from which Shakspere had apparently received suggestions, and instanced one or two cases in which actual peculiarities of phrase in Florio's translation of the Essays are adopted by him, in addition to a peculiar coincidence which has been pointed out by Mr. Jacob Feis in his work entitled Shakspere and Montaigne; and since then the late Mr. Henry Morley, in his edition of the Florio translation, has pointed to a still more remarkable coincidence of phrase, in a passage of Hamlet which I had traced to Montaigne without noticing the decisive verbal agreement in question. Yet so far as I have seen, the matter has passed for little more than a literary curiosity, arousing no new ideas as to Shakspere's mental development. The notable suggestion of Chasles on that head has been ignored more completely than the theory of Mr. Feis, which in comparison is merely fantastic. Either, then, there is an unwillingness in England to conceive of Shakspere as owing much to foreign influences, or as a case of intelligible mental growth, or else the whole critical problem which Shakspere represents—and he may be regarded as the 7 greatest of critical problems—comes within the general disregard for serious criticism, noticeable among us of late years. And the work of Mr. Feis, unfortunately, is as a whole so extravagant that it could hardly fail to bring a special suspicion on every form of the theory of an intellectual tie between Shakspere and Montaigne. Not only does he undertake to show in dead earnest what Sterling had vaguely suggested as conceivable, that Shakspere meant Hamlet to represent Montaigne, but he strenuously argues that the poet framed the play in order to discredit Montaigne's opinions—a thesis which almost makes the Bacon theory specious by comparison. Naturally it has made no converts, even in Germany, where, as it happens, it had been anticipated.

In France, however, the neglect of the special problem of Montaigne's influence on Shakspere is less easily to be explained, seeing how much intelligent study has been given of late by French critics to both Shakspere and Montaigne. The influence is recognised; but here again it is only cursorily traced. The latest study of Montaigne is that of M. Paul Stapfer, 8 a vigilant critic, whose services to Shakspere-study have been recognised in both countries. But all that M. Stapfer claims for the influence of the French essayist on the English dramatist is thus put: —

"Montaigne is perhaps too purely French to have exercised much influence abroad. Nevertheless his influence on England is not to be disdained. Shakspere appreciated him (*le gotait*); he has inserted in the Tempest a passage of the chapter Des Cannibales; and the strong expressions of the Essays on man, the inconstant, irresolute being, contrary to himself, marvellously vain, various and changeful, were perhaps not unconnected with (*peut 꽿e pas 鵬ang航s 네>*) *the conception of Hamlet. The author of the scene of the grave-diggers must have felt the savour and retained the impression of this thought, humid and cold as the grave: 'The heart and the life of a great and triumphant emperor are but the repast of a little worm.' The translation of Plutarch, or rather of Amyot, by Thomas North, and that of Montaigne by Florio, had together a great and long vogue in the English society of the seventeenth century."* 5

So modest a claim, coming from the French side, can hardly be blamed on the score of that very modesty. It is the fact, however, that, though M. Stapfer has in another work 6 com 9 pared Shakspere with a French classic critically enough, he has here understated his case. He was led to such an attitude in his earlier study of Shakspere by the slightness of the evidence offered for the claim of M. Chasles, of which he wrote that it is "a gratuitous supposition, quite unjustified by the few traces in his writings of his having read the Essays." 7 But that verdict was passed without due scrutiny. The influence of Montaigne on Shakspere was both wider and deeper than M. Stapfer has suggested; and it is perhaps more fitting, after all, that the proof should be undertaken by some of us who, speaking Shakspere's tongue, cannot well be suspected of seeking to belittle him when we trace the sources for his thought, whether in his life or in his culture. There is still, indeed, a tendency among the more primitively patriotic to look jealously at such inquiries, as tending to diminish the glory of the worshipped name; but for anyone who is capable of appreciating Shakspere's greatness, there can be no question of iconoclasm in the matter. Shakspere ignorantly adored is a mere dubious mystery; Shaks 10 pere followed up and comprehended, step by step, albeit never wholly revealed, becomes more remarkable, more profoundly interesting, as he becomes more intelligible. We are embarked, not on a quest for plagiarisms, but on a study of the growth of a wonderful mind. And in the idea that much of the growth is traceable to the fertilising contact of a foreign intelligence there can be nothing but interest and attraction for those who have mastered the primary sociological truth that such contacts of cultures are the very life of civilisation.

11

II.

The first requirement in the study, obviously, is an exact statement of the coincidences of phrase and thought in Shakspere and Montaigne. Not that such coincidences are the main or the only results to be looked for; rather we may reasonably expect to find Shakspere's thought often diverging at a tangent from that of the writer he is reading, or even directly gainsaying it. But there can be no solid argument as to such indirect influence until we have fully established the direct influence, and this can only be done by exhibiting a considerable number of coincidences. M. Chasles, while avowing that "the comparison of texts is indispensable – we must undergo this fatigue in order to know to what extent Shakspere, between 1603 and 1615, became familiar with Montaigne" – strangely enough made no comparison of texts whatever beyond reproducing the familiar paraphrase in the Tempest, from the essay Of Cannibals; and left absolutely unsupported his 12 assertion as to Hamlet, Othello, and Coriolanus. It is necessary to produce proofs, and to look narrowly to dates. Florio's translation, though licensed in 1601, was not published till 1603, the year of the piratical publication of the First Quarto of Hamlet, in which the play lacks much of its present matter, and shows in many parts so little trace of Shakspere's spirit and versification that, even if we hold the text to have been imperfectly taken down in shorthand, as it no doubt was, we cannot suppose him to have at this stage completed his refashioning of the older play, which is undoubtedly the substratum of his. 8 We must therefore keep closely in view the divergencies between this text and that of the Second Quarto, printed in 1604, in which the transmuting touch of Shakspere is broadly evident. It is quite possible that Shakspere may have seen parts of Florio's translation before 1603, or heard passages from it read; or even that he might have read Montaigne in the original. But as his possession of the translation is made certain by the preserva 13 tion of the copy bearing his autograph, and as it is from Florio that he is seen to have copied in the passages where his copying is beyond dispute, it is on Florio's translation that we must proceed.

I. In order to keep all the evidence in view, we may first of all collate once more the passage in the Tempest with that in the Essays which it unquestionably follows. In Florio's translation, Montaigne's words run:

"They [Lycurgus and Plato] could not imagine a genuity so pure and simple, as we see it by experience, nor ever believe our society might be maintained with so little art and human combination. It is a nation (would I answer Plato) that hath no kind of traffic, no knowledge of letters, no intelligence of numbers, no name of magistrate, nor of politic superiority; no use of service, of riches, or of poverty; no contracts, no successions, no dividences, no occupations, but idle; no respect of kindred, but common; no apparel, but natural; no manuring of lands, no use of wine, corn, or metal. The very words that import lying, falsehood, treason, dissimulation, covetousness, envy, detraction, and passion, were never heard of amongst them. How dissonant would he find his imaginary commonwealth from this perfection?"

Compare the speech in which the kind old Gonzalo seeks to divert the troubled mind of the shipwrecked King Alonso: 14

> *"I' the commonwealth I would by contraries Execute all things: for no kind of traffic Would I admit; no name of magistrate; Letters should not be known; no use of service, Of riches, or of poverty; no contracts, Succession; bound of land, tilth, vineyard, none: No use of metal, corn, or wine, or oil: No occupation, all men idle, all; And women too: but innocent and pure: No sovereignty...."*

There can be no dispute as to the direct transcription here, where the dramatist is but incidentally playing with Montaigne's idea, proceeding to put some gibes at it in the mouths of Gonzalo's rascally comrades; and it follows that Gonzalo's further phrase, "to excel the golden age," proceeds from Montaigne's previous words: "exceed all the pictures wherewith licentious poesy hath proudly embellished the golden age." The play was in all probability written in or before 1610. It remains to show that on his first reading of Florio's Montaigne, in 1603-4, Shakspere was more deeply and widely influenced, though the specific proofs are in the nature of the case less palpable.

II. Let us take first the more decisive coincidences of phrase. Correspond-ences of thought 15 which in themselves do not establish their direct con-nection, have a new significance when it is seen that other coincidences amount to manifest reproduction. And such a coincidence we have, to begin with, in the familiar lines:

> *"There's a divinity that shapes our ends, Rough-hew them how we will." 9*

I pointed out in 1885 that this expression, which does not occur in the First Quarto Hamlet, corresponds very closely with the theme of Mon-taigne's essay, THAT FORTUNE IS OFTENTIMES MET WITHALL IN PURSUIT OF REASON, 10 in which occurs the phrase, "Fortune has more judgment 11 than we," a translation from Menander. But Professor Morley, having had his attention called to the subject by the work of Mr. Feis, who had suggested another passage as the source of Shakspere's, made a more perfect identification. Reading the proofs of the Florio translation for his reprint, he found, what I had not observed in my occasional access to the old folio, not then reprinted, that the very metaphor of "rough-hewing" occurs in Florio's rendering of a pas 16 sage in the Essays: — 12 "My consultation doth somewhat roughly hew the matter, and by its first shew lightly consider the same: the main and chief point of the work I am wont to resign to Heaven." This is a much more exact coincidence than is presented in the passage cited by Mr. Feis from the essay Of Physiogno-my: — 13 "Therefore do our designs so often miscarry.... The heavens are angry, and I may say envious of the extension and large privilege we as-cribe to human wisdom, to the prejudice of theirs, and abridge them so much more unto us by so much more we endeavour to amplify them." If there were no closer parallel than that in Montaigne, we should be bound to take it as an expansion of a phrase in Seneca's Agamemnon, 14 which was likely to have become proverbial. I may add that the thought is often repeated in the Essays, and that in several passages it compares notably with Shakspere's lines. These begin:

> *"Rashly, — And praised be rashness for it — Let us know Our in-discretion sometimes serves us well 17 When our deep plots do pall; and that should learn us There's a divinity" etc.*

Compare the following extracts from Florio's translation: —

"The Dæmon of Socrates were peradventure a certain inpulsion or will which without the advice of his discourse presented itself unto him. In a mind so well purified, and by continual exercise of wisdom and virtue so well prepared as his was, it is likely his inclinations (though rash and inconsiderate) were ever of great moment, and worthy to be followed. Every man feeleth in himself some image of such agitations, of a prompt, vehement, and casual opinion. It is in me to give them some authority, that afford so little to our wisdom. And I have had some (equally weak in reason and violent in persuasion and dissuasion, which was more ordinary to Socrates) by which I have so happily and so profitably suffered myself to be transported, as they might perhaps be thought to contain some matter of divine inspiration." 15

"Even in our counsels and deliberations, some chance or good luck must needs be joined to them; for whatsoever our wisdom can effect is no great matter." 16

"When I consider the most glorious exploits of war, methinks I see that those who have had the conduct of them employ neither counsel nor deliberation about them, but for fashion sake, and leave the best part of 18 the enterprise to fortune; and on the confidence they have in her aid, they still go beyond the limits of all discourse. Casual rejoicings and strange furies ensue among their deliberations." 17 etc.

Compare finally Florio's translation of the lines of Manilius cited by Montaigne at the end of the 47th Essay of the First Book:

> *"'Tis best for ill-advis'd, wisdom may fail, 18 Fortune proves not the cause that should prevail, But here and there without respect doth sail: A higher power forsooth us overdraws, And mortal states guides with immortal laws."*

It is to be remembered, indeed, that the idea expressed in Hamlet's words to Horatio is partly anticipated in the rhymed speech of the Player-King in the play-scene in Act III., which occurs in the First Quarto:

> *"Our wills, our fates do so contrary run That our devices still are overthrown; Our thoughts are ours, their ends none of our own."*

Such a passage, reiterating a familiar commonplace, might seem at first sight to tell against the view that Hamlet's later speech to Horatio is an echo of Montaigne. But that view being 19 found justified by the evidence, and the idea in that passage being exactly coincident with Montaigne's, while the above lines are only partially parallel in meaning, we are forced to admit that Shakspere may have been influenced by Montaigne even where a partial precedent might be found in his own or other English work.

III. The phrase "discourse of reason," which is spoken by Hamlet in his first soliloquy, 19 and which first appears in the Second Quarto, is not used by Shakspere in any play before Hamlet; and he uses it again in Troilus and Cressida; 20 while "discourse of thought" appears in Othello; 21 and "discourse," in the sense of reasoning faculty, is used in Hamlet's last soliloquy. 22 In English literature this use of the word seems to be special in Shakspere's period, 23 and it has been noted by an admirer as a finely Shaksperean expression. But the expression "discourse of reason" occurs at least four times in Montaigne's Essays, and in Florio's translation 20 of them: in the essay 24 That to philosophise is to learn how to die; again at the close of the essay 25 A demain les affaires; again in the first paragraph of the Apology of Raimond Sebonde 26; and yet again in the chapter on The History of Spurina; 27 and though it seems to be scholastic in origin, and occurs once or twice before 1600 in English books, it is difficult to doubt that, like the other phrase above cited, it came to Shakspere through Florio's Montaigne. The word discours is a hundred times used singly by Montaigne, as by Shakspere in the phrase "of such large discourse," for the process of ratiocination.

IV. Then again there is the clue of Skakspere's use of the word "consummation" in the revised form of the "To be" soliloquy. This, as Mr. Feis pointed out, 28 is the word used by Florio as a rendering of an頄tissement in the speech of Socrates as given by Montaigne in the essay 29 Of Physiognomy. Shakspere makes Hamlet speak of annihilation as "a consumma 21 tion devoutly to be wished." Florio has: "If it (death) be a consummation of one's being, it is also an amendment and entrance into a long and quiet night. We find nothing so sweet in life as a quiet and gentle sleep, and without dreams." Here not only do the words coincide in a peculiar way, but the idea in the two phrases is the same; the theme of sleep and dreams being further common to the two writings.

Beyond these, I have not noted any correspondences of phrase so precise as to prove reminiscence beyond possibility of dispute; but it is not difficult to trace striking correspondences which, though falling short of explicit reproduction, inevitably suggest a relation; and these it now behoves us to *consider. The remarkable thing is, as regards Hamlet, that they almost all occur in passages not present in the First Quarto.*

V. When we compare part of the speech of Rosencrantz on sedition 30 with a passage in Montaigne's essay, Of Custom, 31 we find a somewhat close coincidence. In the play Rosencrantz says:

22

> *"The cease of Majesty, Dies not alone; but like a gulf doth draw What's near with it: it is a massy wheel Fix'd on the summit of the highest mount, To whose huge spokes ten thousand lesser things Are mortised and adjoined; which, when it falls, Each small an-nexment, petty consequence, Attends the boisterous ruin."*

Florio has:

"Those who attempt to shake an Estate are commonly the first over-thrown by the fall of it.... The contexture and combining of this monarchy and great building having been dismissed and dissolved by it, namely, in her old years, giveth as much overture and entrance as a man will to like injuries. Royal majesty doth more hardly fall from the top to the middle, than it tumbleth down from the middle to the bottom."

The verbal correspondence here is only less decisive — as regards the use of the word "majesty" — than in the passages collated by Mr. Morley; while the thought corresponds as closely.

VI. The speech of Hamlet, 32 "There is nothing either good or bad but thinking makes it so"; and Iago's "'tis in ourselves that we are thus or thus," 33 are expressions of a favourite 23 thesis of Montaigne's, to which he devotes an entire essay. 34 The Shaksperean phrases echo closely such sentences as: —

"If that which we call evil and torment be neither torment nor evil, but that our fancy only gives it that quality, it is in us to change it.... That which we term evil is not so of itself."... "Every man is either well or ill according as he finds himself."

And in the essay 35 Of Democritus and Heraclitus there is another close parallel: —

"Therefore let us take no more excuses from external qualities of things. To us it belongeth to give ourselves account of it. Our good and our evil hath no dependency but from ourselves."

VII. Hamlet's apostrophe to his mother on the power of custom — a passage which, like the others above cited, first appears in the Second Quarto — is similarly an echo of a favourite proposition of Montaigne, who devotes to it the essay 36 Of Custom, and not to change readily a received law. In that there occur the typical passages: —

"Custom doth so blear us that we cannot distinguish the usage of things.... Certes, chastity is an ex 24 cellent virtue, the commodity whereof is very well known; but to use it, and according to nature to prevail with it, is as hard as it is easy to endear it and to prevail with it according to custom, to laws and precepts." "The laws of conscience, which we say are born of nature, are born of custom."

Again, in the essay Of Controlling one's Will 37 we have: "Custom is a second nature, and not less potent."

Hamlet's words are: —

> *"That monster, custom, who all sense doth eat Of habits devil, is angel yet in this That to the use of actions fair and good He likewise gives a frock or livery That aptly is put on.... For use can almost change the stamp of nature."*

No doubt the idea is a classic commonplace; and in the early Two Gentlemen of Verona 38 we actually have the line, "How use doth breed a habit in a man;" but here again there seems reason to regard Montaigne as having suggested Shakspere's vivid and many-coloured wording of the idea in the tragedy. Indeed, even the line cited from the early comedy may have been one of the poet's many later additions to his text.

25

VIII. A less close but still a noteworthy resemblance is that between the passage in which Hamlet expresses to Rosencrantz and Guildenstern the veering of his mood from joy in things to disgust with them, and the paragraph in the Apology of Raimond Sebonde in which Montaigne sets against each other the splendour of the universe and the littleness of man. Here the thought diverges, Shakspere making it his own as he always does, and altering its aim; but the language is curiously similar. Hamlet says:

"It goes so heavily with my disposition that this goodly frame, the earth, seems to me a sterile promontory: this most excellent canopy, the air, look you, this brave o'erhanging firmament, this majestical roof, fretted with golden fire, why it appears no other thing to me than a foul and pestilent congregation of vapours. What a piece of work is man! How noble in reason! how infinite in faculties! in form and moving, how express and admirable! in action, how like an angel! in apprehension, how like a God! the beauty of the world! the paragon of animals! And yet to me what is this quintessence of dust? Man delights not me."

Montaigne, as translated by Florio, has:

"Let us see what hold-fast or free-hold he (man) hath in this gorgeous and goodly equipage.... Who hath persuaded him, that this admirable moving of 26 heaven's vaults, that the eternal light of these lamps so fiercely rolling over his head ... were established ... for his commodity and service? Is it possible to imagine anything so ridiculous as this miserable and wretched creature, which is not so much as master of himself, exposed and subject to offences of all things, and yet dareth call himself Master and Emperor of this universe?... [To consider ... the power and domination these (celestial) bodies have, not only upon our lives and conditions of our fortune ... but also over our dispositions and inclinations, our discourses and wills, which they rule, provoke, and move at the pleasure of their influences.]... Of all creatures man is the most miserable and frail, and therewithal the proudest and disdainfullest. Who perceiveth himself placed here, amidst the filth and mire of the world ... and yet dareth imaginarily place himself above the circle of the Moon, and reduce heaven under his feet. It is through the vanity of the same imagination that he dare equal himself to God."

The passage in brackets is left here in its place, not as suggesting anything in Hamlet's speech, but as paralleling a line in Measure for Measure, to be dealt with immediately. But it will be seen that the rest of the passage, though turned to quite another purpose than Hamlet's, brings together in the same way a set of contrasted ideas of human greatness and smallness, and of the splendour of the midnight firmament. 39

27 IX. The nervous protest of Hamlet to Horatio on the point of the national vice of drunkenness, 40 of which all save the beginning is added in the Second Quarto just before the entrance of the Ghost, has several curious points of coincidence with Montaigne's essay 41 on The History of Spurina, which discusses at great length a matter of special interest to

Shakspere — the character of Julius Cæsar. In the course of the examination Montaigne takes trouble to show that Cato's use of the epithet "drunkard" to Cæsar could not have been meant literally; that the same Cato admitted Cæsar's sobriety in the matter of drinking. It is after making light of Cæsar's faults in other matters of personal conduct that the essayist comes to this decision:

"But all these noble inclinations, rich gifts, worthy qualities, were altered, smothered, and eclipsed by this furious passion of ambition.... To conclude, this 28 only vice (in mine opinion) lost and overthrew in him the fairest natural and richest ingenuity that ever was, and hath made his memory abominable to all honest minds."

Compare the exquisitely high-strung lines, so congruous in their excited rapidity with Hamlet's intensity of expectation, which follow on his notable outburst on the subject of drunkenness:

> *"So oft it chances in particular men, That for some vicious mode of nature in them, As in their birth (wherein they are not guilty, Since nature cannot choose its origin), By the o'ergrowth of some complexion, Oft breaking down the pales and forts of reason; Or by some habit that too much o'er-leavens The form of plausive manners; that these men, — Carrying, I say, the stamp of one defect; Being nature's livery, or fortune's star, — Their virtues else (be they as pure as grace, As infinite as man may undergo) Shall in the general censure take corruption From that particular fault...."*

Even the idea that "nature cannot choose its origin" is suggested by the context in Montaigne. 42 Shakspere's estimate of Cæsar, of course, diverged from that of the essay.

29 X. I find a certain singularity of coincidence between the words of King Claudius on kingship:

> *"There's such divinity doth hedge a king, That treason can but peep to what it would, Acts little of his will,"*

and a passage in the essay 43 Of the Incommodity of Greatness:

"To be a king, is a matter of that consequence, that only by it he is so. That strange glimmering and eye-dazzling light, which round about envi-

roneth, over-casteth and hideth from us: our weak sight is thereby bleared and dissipated, as being filled and obscured by that greater and further-spreading brightness."

The working out of the metaphor here gives at once to Shakspere's terms "divinity" and "can but peep" a point not otherwise easily seen; but the idea of a dazzling light may be really what was meant in the play; and one is tempted to pronounce the passage a reminiscence of Montaigne. Here, 30 however, it has to be noted that in the First Quarto we have the lines:

> *"There's such divinity doth wall a king That treason dares not look on."*

And if Shakspere had not seen or heard the passage in Montaigne before the publication of Florio's folio — which, however, he may very well have done — the theory of reminiscence here cannot stand.

XI. In Hamlet's soliloquy on the passage of the army of Fortinbras — one of the many passages added in the Second Quarto — there is a strong general resemblance to a passage in the essay Of Diversion. 44 Hamlet first remarks to the Captain:

> *"Two thousand souls and twenty thousand ducats Will not debate the question of this straw: This is the imposthume of much wealth and peace;"*

and afterwards soliloquises:

> *"Examples gross as earth exhort me: Witness, this army of such mass and charge, Led by a delicate and tender prince, Whose spirit, by divine ambition puff'd, Makes mouths at the invisible event; Exposing what is mortal and unsure 31 To all that fortune, death, and danger dare, Even for an egg-shell. Rightly to be great, Is not to stir without great argument, But greatly to find quarrel in a straw. When honour is at stake....*
>
> *....to my shame I see The imminent death of twenty thousand men, That for a fantasy and trick of fame, Go to their graves like beds; fight for a plot Whereon the numbers cannot try the cause...."*

Montaigne has the same general idea in the essay Of Diversion:

"If one demand that fellow, what interest he hath in such a siege: The interest of example (he will say) and common obedience of the Prince: I nor look nor pretend any benefit thereby ... I have neither passion nor quarrel in the matter. Yet the next day you will see him all changed, and chafing, boiling and blushing with rage, in his rank of battle, ready for the assault. It is the glaring reflecting of so much steel, the flashing thundering of the cannon, the clang of trumpets, and the rattling of drums, that have infused this new fury and rancour in his swelling veins. A frivolous cause, will you say? How a cause? There needeth none to excite our mind. A doting humour without body, without substance, overswayeth it up and down."

The thought recurs in the essay, Of Controlling one's Will. 45

32 "Our greatest agitations have strange springs and ridiculous causes. What ruin did our last Duke of Burgundy run into, for the quarrel of a cart-load of sheep-skins?... See why that man doth hazard both his honour and life on the fortune of his rapier and dagger; let him tell you whence the cause of that confusion ariseth, he cannot without blushing; so vain and frivolous is the occasion."

And the idea in Hamlet's lines "rightly to be great," etc., is suggested in the essay Of Repenting, 46 where we have:

"The nearest way to come unto glory were to do that for conscience which we do for glory.... The worth of the mind consisteth not in going high, but in going orderly. Her greatness is not exercised in greatness; in mediocrity it is."

In the essay Of Experience 47 there is a sentence partially expressing the same thought, which is cited by Mr. Feis as a reproduction:

"The greatness of the mind is not so much to draw up, and hale forward, as to know how to range, direct, and circumscribe itself. It holdeth for great what is sufficient, and sheweth her height in loving mean things better than eminent."

Here, certainly, as in the previous citation, the idea is not identical with that expressed by Hamlet. But the elements he combines are 33 there; and again, in the essay Of Solitariness 48 we have the picture of the soldier fighting furiously for the quarrel of his careless king, with the question: "Who doth not willingly chop and counter-change his health, his ease, yea his life, for glory and reputation, the most unprofitable, vain, and counterfeit coin that is in use with us."

And yet again the thought crops up in the Apology of Raimond Sebonde:

"This horror-causing array of so many thousands of armed men, so great fury, earnest fervour, and undaunted courage, it would make one laugh to see on how many vain occasions it is raised and set on fire.... The hatred of one man, a spite, a pleasure ... causes which ought not to move two scolding fishwives to catch one another, is the soul and motive of all this hurly-burly."

XII. Yet one more of Hamlet's sayings peculiar to the revised form of the play seems to be an echo of a thought of Montaigne's. At the outset of the soliloquy last quoted from, Hamlet says:—

> *"What is a man If his chief good and market of his time, 34 Be but to sleep and feed? A beast; no more. Sure He that made us with such large discourse, Looking before and after, gave us not That capability and godlike reason To fust in us unused."*

The bearing of the thought in the soliloquy, where Hamlet spasmodically applies it to the stimulation of his vengeance, is certainly never given to it by Montaigne, who has left on record 49 his small approbation of revenge; but the thought itself is there, in the essay 50 On Goods and Evils.

"Shall we employ the intelligence Heaven hath bestowed upon us for our greatest good, to our ruin, repugning nature's design and the universal order and vicissitude of things, which implieth that every man should use his instrument and means for his own commodity?"

Again, there is a passage in the essay Of the Affection of Fathers to their Children, 51 where there occurs a specific coincidence of phrase, the special use of the term "discourse," which we have already traced from Shakspere to Montaigne; and where at the same time the contrast between man and beast is drawn, though 35 not to the same purpose as in the speech of Hamlet:—

"Since it hath pleased God to endow us with some capacity of discourse, that as beasts we should not servilely be subjected to common laws, but rather with judgment and voluntary liberty apply ourselves unto them, we ought somewhat to yield unto the simple authority of Nature, but not suffer her tyrannically to carry us away; only reason ought to have the conduct of our inclinations."

Finally we have a third parallel, with a slight coincidence of terms, in the essay 52 Of Giving the lie:

"Nature hath endowed us with a large faculty to entertain ourselves apart, and often calleth us unto it, to teach us that partly we owe ourselves unto society, but in the better part unto ourselves."

It may be argued that these, like one or two of the other sayings above cited as echoed by Shakspere from Montaigne, are of the nature of general religious or ethical maxims, traceable to no one source; and if we only found one or two such parallels, their resemblance of course would have no evidential value, save as regards coincidence of terms. For this very passage, for 36 instance, there is a classic original, or at least a familiar source, in Cicero, 53 where the commonplace of the contrast between man and beast is drawn in terms that come in a general way pretty close to Hamlet's. This treatise of Cicero was available to Shakspere in several English translations; 54 and only the fact that we find no general trace of Cicero in the play entitles us to suggest a connection in this special case with Montaigne, of whom we do find so many other traces. It is easy besides to push the theory of any influence too far; and when for instance we find Hamlet saying he fares "Of the chameleon's dish: I eat the air, promise-crammed," it would be as idle to assume a reminiscence of a passage of Montaigne on the chameleon 55 as it would be to derive Hamlet's phrase "A king of shreds and patches" from Florio's rendering in the essay 56 Of the Inconstancy of our Actions:

"We are all framed of flaps and patches, and of so shapeless and diverse a contexture, that every piece and every moment playeth his part."

37

In the latter case we have a mere coincidence of idiom; in the former a proverbial allusion. 57 An uncritical pursuit of such mere accidents of resemblance has led Mr. Feis to such enormities as the assertion that Shakspere's contemporaries knew Hamlet's use of his tablets to be a parody of the "much-scribbling Montaigne," who had avowed that he made much use of his; the assertion that Ophelia's "Come, my coach!" has reference to Montaigne's remark that he has known ladies who would rather lend their honour than their coach; and a dozen other propositions, if possible still more amazing. But when, with no foregone conclusion as to any polemic purpose on Shakspere's part, we restrict ourselves to real parallels of thought and expression; when we find that a certain number of these are actually textual; when we find further that in a single soliloquy in the 38 play there are several reproductions of ideas in the essays, some of them frequently recurring in Montaigne; and when finally it is found that, with only one exception, all the passages in question have been added to the play in the Second Quarto, after the publication of Florio's translation, it seems hardly possible to doubt that the translation influenced the dramatist in his work.

Needless to say, the influence is from the very start of that high sort in which he that takes becomes co-thinker with him that gives, Shakspere's absorption of Montaigne being as vital as Montaigne's own assimilation of the thought of his classics. The process is one not of surface reflection, but of kindling by contact; and we seem to see even the vibration of the style passing from one intelligence to the other; the nervous and copious speech of Montaigne awakening Shakspere to a new sense of power over rhythm and poignant phrase, at the same time that the stimulus of the thought gives him a new confidence in the validity of his own reflection. Some cause there must have been for this marked species of development in the dramatist 39 at that particular time; and if we find pervading signs of one remarkable new influence, with no countervailing evidence of another adequate to the effect, the inference is about as reasonable as many which pass for valid in astronomy. For it will be found, on the one hand, that there is no sign worth considering of a Montaigne influence on Shakspere before Hamlet; and, on the other hand, that the influence to some extent continues beyond that play. Indeed, there are still further minute signs of it there, which should be noted before we pass on.

XIII. Among parallelisms of thought of a less direct kind, one may be traced between an utterance of Hamlet's and a number of Montaigne's sayings on the power of imagination and the possible equivalence of dream life and waking life. In his first dialogue with Rosencrantz and Guildenstern, where we have already noted an echo of Montaigne, Hamlet cries:

"O God! I could be bounded in a nutshell, and count myself a king of infinite space; were it not that I have bad dreams;"

and Guildenstern answers:

"Which dreams, indeed, are ambition; for the very substance of the ambitious is merely the shadow of a dream."

40

The first sentence may be compared with a number in Montaigne, 58 of which the following 59 is a type:

"Man clean contrary [to the Gods] possesseth goods in imagination and evils essentially. We have had reason to make the powers of our imagina-

tion to be of force, for all our felicities are but in conceipt, and as it were in a dream;"

while the reply of Guildenstern further recalls several of the passages already cited.

XIV. Another apparent parallel of no great importance, but of more verbal closeness, is that between Hamlet's jeering phrase: 60 "Your worm is your only emperor for diet," and a sentence in the Apology: "The heart and the life of a great and triumphant emperor are the dinner of a little worm," which M. Stapfer compares further with the talk of Hamlet in the grave-diggers' scene. Here, doubtless, we are near the level of proverbial sayings, current in all countries.

XV. As regards Hamlet, I can find no further parallelisms so direct as any of the foregoing, except some to be considered later, in con 41 nection with the "To be" soliloquy. I do not think it can be made out that, as M. Chasles affirmed, Hamlet's words on his friendship for Horatio can be traced directly to any of Montaigne's passages on that theme. "It would be easy," says M. Chasles, "to show in Shakspere the branloire perenne 61 of Montaigne, and the whole magnificent passage on friendship, which is found reproduced (se trouve report廳>) in Hamlet." The idea of the world as a perpetual mutation is certainly prevalent in Shakspere's work; but I can find no exact correspondence of phrase between Montaigne's pages on his love for his dead friend Etienne de la Bo볼e and the lines in which Hamlet speaks of his love for Horatio. He rather gives his reasons for his love than describes the nature and completeness of it in Montaigne's way; and as regards the description of Horatio, it could have been independently suggested by such a treatise as Seneca's De Constantia Sapientis, which is a monody on the theme with which it closes: esse aliquem invictum, esse aliquem in quem nihil 42 fortuna possit – "to be something unconquered, something against which fortune is powerless." In the fifth section the idea is worded in a fashion that could have suggested Shakspere's utterance of it; and he might easily have met with some citation of the kind. But, on the other hand, this note of passionate friendship is not only new in Shakspere but new in Hamlet, in respect of the First Quarto, in which the main part of the speech to Horatio does not occur, and in view of the singular fact that in the first Act of the play as it stands Hamlet greets Horatio as a mere acquaintance; and it is further to be noted that the description of Horatio as "one in suffering all that suffers nothing" is broadly suggested by the quotation from Horace in Montaigne's nineteenth chapter (which, as we have already seen, impressed Shakspere), and by various other sayings in the Essays. After the quotation from Horace (Non vultus instantis tyranni), in the Nineteenth Essay, Florio's translation runs:

"She (the soul) is made mistress of her passions and concupiscences, lady of indigence, of shame, of poverty, and of all fortune's injuries. Let him that can, attain 43 to this advantage. Herein consists the true and sovereign liberty, that affords us means wherewith to jest and make a scorn of force and injustice, and to deride imprisonment, gyves, or fetters."

Again, in the essay Of Three Commerces or Societies, 62 we have this:

"We must not cleave so fast unto our humours and dispositions. Our chiefest sufficiency is to supply ourselves to diverse fashions. It is a being, but not a life, to be tied and bound by necessity to one only course. The goodliest minds are those that have most variety and pliableness in them.... Life is a motion unequal, irregular, and multiform....

"... My fortune having inured and allured me, even from my infancy, to one sole, singular, and perfect amity, hath verily in some sort distasted me from others.... So that it is naturally a pain unto me to communicate myself by halves, and with modification....

"I should commend a high-raised mind that could both bend and discharge itself; that wherever her fortune might transport her, she might continue constant.... I envy those which can be familiar with the meanest of their followers, and vouchsafe to contract friendship and frame discourse with their own servants."

Again, la Boétie is panegyrised by Montaigne for his rare poise and firmness of character; 63 44 and elsewhere in the essays we find many allusions to the ideal of the imperturbable man, which Montaigne has in the above cited passages brought into connection with his ideal of friendship. It could well be, then — though here we cannot argue the point with confidence — that in this as in other matters the strong general impression that Montaigne was so well fitted to make on Shakspere's mind was the source of such a change in the conception and exposition of Hamlet's relation to Horatio as is set up by Hamlet's protestation of his long-standing admiration and love for his friend. Shakspere's own relations with one or other of his noble patrons would make him specially alive to such suggestion.

XVI. We now come to the suggested resemblance between the "To be or not to be" soliloquy and the general tone of Montaigne on the subject of death. On this resemblance I am less disposed to lay stress now than I was on a first consideration of the subject thirteen years ago. While I find new coincidences of detail on a more systematic search, I am less impressed by the alleged general resemblance of tone. In point of fact, the general drift of Hamlet's 45 soliloquy is rather alien to the general tone of Montaigne on the same theme. That tone, as we shall see, harmonises much more nearly with the speech of the Duke to Claudio, on the same theme, in Measure for Measure. What really seems to subsist in the "To be" soliloquy, after a careful scrutiny, is a series of echoes of single thoughts; but there is the difficulty that some of these occur in the earlier form of the soliloquy in the First Quarto, a circumstance which tends — though not necessarily 64 — to throw a shade of doubt on the apparent echoes in the finished form of the speech. We can but weigh the facts as impartially as may be.

First, there is the striking coincidence of the word "consummation" (which appears only in the Second Quarto), with Florio's translation of an 額tissement in the essay Of Physiognomy, as above noted. Secondly, there is a curious resemblance between the phrase "take arms against a sea of troubles" and a passage in Florio's version of the same essay, which has somehow been 46 overlooked in the disputes over Shakspere's line. It runs:

"I sometimes suffer myself by starts to be surprised with the pinchings of these unpleasant conceits, which, whilst I arm myself to expel or wrestle against them, assail and beat me. Lo here another huddle or tide of mischief, that on the neck of the former came rushing upon me."

There arises here the difficulty that Shakspere's line had been satisfactorily traced to Tian's 65 story of the Celtic practice of rushing into the sea to resist a high tide with weapons; and the matter must, I think, be left open until it can he ascertained whether the statement concerning the Celts was available to Shakspere in any translation or citation. 66

Again, the phrase "Conscience doth make cowards of us all" is very like the echo of two passages in the essay 67 Of Conscience: "Of such marvellous working power is the sting of conscience: which often induceth us to bewray, to accuse, and to combat ourselves"; "which as it doth fill us with fear and doubt, so doth it 47 store us with assurance and trust;" and the lines about "the dread of something after death" might point to the passage in the Fortieth Essay, in which Montaigne cites the saying of Augustine that "Nothing but what follows death, makes death to be evil" (malam mortem non facit, nisi quod sequitur mortem) cited by Montaigne in order to dispute it. The same thought, too, is dealt with in the essay 68 on A

Custom of the Isle of Cea, which contains a passage suggestive of Hamlet's earlier soliloquy on self-slaughter. But, for one thing, Hamlet's soliloquies are contrary in drift to Montaigne's argument; and, for another, the phrase "Conscience makes cowards of us all" existed in the soliloquy as it stood in the First Quarto, while the gist of the idea is actually found twice in a previous play, where it has a proverbial ring. 69 And "the hope of something after death" figures in the First Quarto also.

Finally, there are other sources than Montaigne for parts of the soliloquy, sources nearer, too, than those which have been pointed to in 48 the Senecan tragedies. There is, indeed, as Dr. Cunliffe has pointed out, 70 a broad correspondence between the whole soliloquy and the chorus of women at the end of the second Act of the Troades, where the question of a life beyond is pointedly put:

> *"Verum est? an timidos fabula decepit, Umbras corporibus vivere conditis?"*

It is true that the choristers in Seneca pronounce definitely against the future life:

> *"Post mortem nihil est, ipsaque mors nihil.... Rumores vacui verbaque inania, Et par sollicito fabula somnio."*

But wherever in Christendom the pagan's words were discussed, the Christian hypothesis would be pitted against his unbelief, with the effect of making one thought overlay the other; and in this fused form the discussion may easily have reached Shakspere's eye and ear. So it would be with the echo of two Senecan passages noted by Mr. Munro in the verses on "the undiscovered country from whose bourn no traveller returns." In the Hercules Furens 71 we have:

> *"Nemo ad id sero venit, unde nunquam Quum semel venit potuit reverti;"*

49

and in the Hercules Œt浔 72 there is the same thought:

> *"regnum canis inquieti Unde non unquam remeavit ullus."*

But here, as elsewhere, Seneca himself was employing a standing senti-ment, for in the best known poem of Catullus we have:

"Qui nunc it per iter tenebricosum Illuc, unde negant redire quemquam." 73

And though there was in Shakspere's day no English translation of Catullus, the commentators long ago noted 74 that in Sandford's translation of Cornelius Agrippa (? 1569), there occurs the phrase, "The countrie of the dead is irremeable, that they cannot return," a fuller parallel to the passage in the soliloquy than anything cited from the classics.

Finally, in Marlowe's Edward II., 75 written before 1593, we have:

"Weep not for Mortimer, That scorns the world, and, as a traveller, Goes to discover countries yet unknown." 76

50

So that, without going to the Latin, we have obvious English sources for notable parts of the soliloquy.

Thus, though Shakspere may (1) have seen part of the Florio translation, or separate translations of some of the essays, before the issue of the First Quarto; or may (2) easily have heard that very point discussed by Florio, who was the friend of his friend Jonson, or by those who had read the original; or may even (3) himself have read in the original; and though further it seems quite certain that his "consummation devoutly to be wished" was an echo of Florio's translation of the Apology of Socrates; on the other hand we are not entitled to trace the soliloquy as a whole to Montaigne's stimulation of Shakspere's thought. That Shakspere read Montaigne in the original once seemed probable to me, as to others; but, on closer study, I consider it unlikely, were it only because the Montaigne influence in his work begins, as aforesaid, in Hamlet. Of all the apparent coincidences I have noticed between Shakspere's previous plays and the essays, none has any evidential value. (1) The passage on the music of the spheres in 51 the Merchant of Venice 77 recalls the passage on the subject in Montaigne's essay of Custom; 78 but then the original source is Cicero, In Somnium Scipionis, which had been translated into English in 1577. (2) Falstaff's rhapsody on the virtues of sherris 79 recalls a passage in the essay of Drunkenness, 80 but then Montaigne avows that what he says is the com-

mon doctrine of wine-drinkers. (3) Montaigne cites 81 the old saying of Petronius, that "all the world's a stage," which occurs in As You Like It; but the phrase itself, being preserved by John of Salisbury, would be current in England. It is, indeed, said to have been the motto of the Globe Theatre. Thus, while we are the more strongly convinced of a Montaigne influence beginning with Hamlet, we are bound to concede the doubtfulness of any apparent influence before the Second Quarto. At most we may say that both of Hamlet's soliloquies which touch on suicide evidently owe something to the discussions set up by Montaigne's essays. 82

52

XVII. In the case of the Duke's exhortation to Claudio in Measure for Measure, on the contrary, the whole speech may be said to be a synthesis of favourite propositions of Montaigne. The thought in itself, of course, is not new or out-of-the-way; it is nearly all to be found suggested in the Latin classics; but in the light of what is certain for us as to Shakspere's study of Montaigne, and of the whole cast of the expression, it is difficult to doubt that Montaigne is for Shakspere the source. Let us take a number of passages from Florio's translation of the Nineteenth Essay, to begin with:

"The end of our career is death: it is the necessary object of our aim; if it affright us, how is it possible we should step one foot further without an ague?"

"What hath an aged man left him of his youth's vigour, and of his fore past life?... When youth fails in us, we feel, nay we perceive, no shaking or transchange at all in ourselves: which is essence and verity is a harder death than that of a languishing and irksome life, or that of age. Forasmuch as the leap from an ill being into a not being is not so dangerous or steepy as it is from a delightful and flourishing being into a painful and sorrowful condition. A weak bending and faint stopping body hath less strength to 53 bear and undergo a heavy burden: So hath our soul."

"Our religion hath no surer human foundation than the contempt of life. Discourse of reason doth not only call and summon us unto it. For why should we fear to lose a thing, which being lost, cannot be moaned? But also, since we are threatened by so many kinds of death, there is no more inconvenience to fear them all than to endure one: what matter it when it cometh, since it is unavoidable?... Death is a part of yourselves; you fly from yourselves. The being you enjoy is equally shared between life and death ... The continual work of your life is to contrive death; you are in

death during the time you continue in life ... during life you are still dying."

The same line of expostulation occurs in other essays. In the Fortieth we have:

"Now death, which some of all horrible things call the most horrible, who knows not how others call it the only haven of this life's torments? the sovereign good of nature? the only stay of our liberty? and the ready and common receipt of our evils?...

"... Death is but felt by discourse, because it is the emotion of an instant. A thousand beasts, a thousand men, are sooner dead than threatened."

Then take a passage occurring near the end of the Apology of Raimond Sebonde:

"We do foolishly fear a kind of death, whereas we have already passed and daily pass so many others.... The flower of age dieth, fadeth, and fleeteth, when age comes upon us, and youth endeth in the 54 flower of a full-grown man's age, childhood in youth, and the first age dieth in infancy; and yesterday endeth in this day, and to-day shall die in to-morrow."

Now compare textually the Duke's speech:

> *"Be absolute for death: either death or life Shall thereby be the sweeter. Reason thus with life: — If I do lose thee, I do lose a thing That none but fools would keep: a breath thou art, (Servile to all the skiey influences) That dost this habitation, where thou keep'st, Hourly afflict: merely, thou are death's fool; For him thou labour'st by thy flight to shun, And yet run'st towards him still: Thou art not noble; For all the accommodations that thou bear'st Are nursed by baseness: Thou art by no means valiant, For thou dost fear the soft and tender fork Of a poor worm: Thy best of rest is sleep, And that thou oft provok'st; yet grossly fear'st Thy death, which is no more. Thou art not thyself; For thou exist'st on many thousand grains Which issue out of dust: Happy thou art not; For what thou hast not, still thou striv'st to get, And what thou hast forget'st: Thou art not certain, For thy complexion shifts to strange effects, After the moon: If thou art rich, thou art poor; For, like an ass whose back with ingots bows, Thou bear'st thy heavy riches but a journey, And death unloads thee: Friend hast thou none; For thine own bowels, which do call thee sire, 55 Do curse the gout, serpigo, and the rheum, For ending thee no sooner: Thou hast no youth nor*

age, But, as it were, an after-dinner's sleep, Dreaming on both: for all thy blessed youth Becomes as aged, and doth beg the alms Of palsied eld; and when thou art old and rich, Thou hast neither heat, affection, limbs, nor beauty, To make thy riches pleasant. What's yet in this, That bears the name of life? Yet in this life Lie hid more thousand deaths: yet death we fear, That makes these odds all even." 83

Then collate yet further some more passages from the Essays:

"They perceived her (the soul) to be capable of diverse passions, and agitated by many languishing and painful motions ... subject to her infirmities, diseases, and offences, even as the stomach or the foot ... dazzled and troubled by the force of wine; removed from her seat by the vapours of a burning fever.... She was seen to dismay and confound all her faculties by the only biting of a sick dog, and to contain no great constancy of discourse, no virtue, no philosophical resolution, no contention of her forces, that might exempt her from the subjection of these accidents...." 84

56

"It is not without reason we are taught to take notice of our sleep, for the resemblance it hath with death. How easily we pass from waking to sleeping; with how little interest we lose the knowledge of light, and of ourselves...." 85

"Wherefore as we from that instant take a title of being, which is but a twinkling in the infinite course of an eternal night, and so short an interruption of our perpetual and natural condition, death possessing whatever is before and behind this moment, and also a good part of this moment, " 86

"Every human nature is ever in the middle between being born and dying, giving nothing of itself but an obscure appearance and shadow, and an uncertain and weak opinion." 87

Compare finally the line "Thy best of rest is sleep" (where the word rest seems a printer's error) with the passage "We find nothing so sweet in life as a quiet and gentle sleep," already cited in connection with our fourth parallel.

XVIII. The theme, in fine, is one of Montaigne's favourites. And the view that Shakspere had been impressed by it seems to be decisively corrob-

orated by the fact that the speech of Claudio to Isabella, expressing those fears of death which the Duke seeks to calm, is 57 likewise an echo of a whole series of passages in Montaigne. Shakspere's lines run:

> "Ay, but to die, and go we know not where, To lie in cold obstruction and to rot: This sensible warm motion to become A kneaded clod; and the delighted spirit To bathe in fiery floods or to reside In thrilling regions of thick-ribbed ice, To be imprisoned in the viewless winds, And blown with restless violence round about The pendent world; or to be worse than worst Of those, that lawless and incertain thoughts Imagine howling! — 'tis too horrible!..."

So far as I know, the only idea in this passage which belongs to the current English superstition of Shakspere's day, apart from the natural notion of death as a mere rotting of the body, is that of the purgatorial fire; unless we assume that the common superstition as to the souls of unbaptised children being blown about until the day of judgment was extended in the popular imagination to the case of executed criminals. He may have heard of the account given by Empedocles, as cited in Plutarch, 88 of the punishment of the offending dæmns, who were whirled between earth and air and sun and sea; but 58 there is no suggestion in that passage that human souls were so treated. Dante's Inferno, with its pictures of carnal sinners tossed about by the winds in the dark air of the second circle, 89 and of traitors punished by freezing in the ninth, 90 was probably not known to the dramatist; nor does Dante's vision coincide with Claudio's, in which the souls are blown "about the pendent world." Shakspere may indeed have heard some of the old tales of a hot and cold purgatory, such as that of Drithelm, given by Bede, 91 whence (rather than from Dante) Milton drew his idea of an alternate torture. 92 But there again, the correspondence is only partial; whereas in Montaigne's Apology of Raimond Sebonde we find, poetry apart, nearly every notion that enters into Claudio's speech:

"The most universal and received fantasy, and which endureth to this day, hath been that whereof Pythagoras is made author ... which is that souls at their departure from us did but pass and roll from one to another body, from a lion to a horse, from a horse 59 to a king, incessantly wandering up and down, from house to mansion.... Some added more, that the same souls do sometimes ascend up to heaven, and come down again.... Origen waked them eternally, to go and come from a good to a bad estate. The opinion that Varro reporteth is, that in the revolutions of four hundred *and forty years they reconjoin themselves unto their first bodies.... Behold her (the soul's) progress elsewhere: He that hath lived well reconjoineth himself unto that star or planet to which he is assigned; who evil, passeth into a woman. And if then he amend not himself, he transchangeth himself into a beast, of condition agreeing to his vicious customs, and shall never see an end of his punishments until ... by virtue of reason he have deprived himself of those gross, stupid, and elementary qualities that were in him.... They (the Epicureans) demand, what order there should be if the throng of the dying should be greater than that of such as be born ... and demand besides, what they should pass their time about, whilst they should stay, until any other mansion were made ready for them.... Others have staved the soul in the deceased bodies, wherewith to animate serpents, worms, and other beasts, which are said to engender from the corruption of our members, yea, and from our ashes.... Others make it immortal without any science or knowledge. Nay, there are some of ours who have deemed that of condemned men's souls devils were made...." 93*

It is at a short distance from this passage that we find the suggestion of a frozen purgatory:

60

"Amongst them (barbarous nations) was also found the belief of purgatory, but after a new form, for what we ascribe unto fire they impute unto cold, and imagine that souls are both purged and punished by the vigor of an extreme coldness." 94

And over and above this peculiar correspondence between the Essays and the two speeches on death, we may note how some of the lines of the Duke in the opening scene connect with two of the passages above cited in connection with Hamlet's last soliloquy, expressing the idea that nature or deity confers gifts in order that they should be used. The Duke's lines are among Shakspere's best:

> *"Thyself and thy belongings Are not thine own so proper as to waste Thyself upon thy virtues, them on thee. Heaven doth with us as we with torches do, Not light them for themselves: for if our virtues Did not go forth of us, 'twere all alike As if we had them not. Spirits are not finely touched But to fine issues: nor nature never lends The smallest scruple of her excellence, But, like a thrifty goddess, she determines Herself the glory of a creditor, Both thanks and use...."*

Here we have once more a characteristically 61 Shaksperean transmutation and development of the idea rather than a reproduction; and the same appears when we compare the admirable lines of the poet with a homiletic sentence from the Apology of Raimond Sebonde: —

"It is not enough for us to serve God in spirit and soul; we owe him besides and we yield unto him a corporal worshipping: we apply our limbs, our motions, and all external things to honour him."

But granting the philosophic as well as the poetic heightening, we are still led to infer a stimulation of the poet's thought by the Essays — a stimulation not limited to one play, but affecting other plays written about the same time. Another point of connection between Hamlet and Measure for Measure is seen when we compare the above passage, "Spirits are not finely touched but to fine issues," with Laertes' lines 95:

> *"Nature is fine in love, and when 'tis fine It sends some precious instance of itself After the thing it loves."*

And though such data are of course not conclusive as to the time of composition of the plays, there is so much of identity between the 62 thought in the Duke's speech, just quoted, and a notable passage in Troilus and Cressida, as to strengthen greatly the surmise that the latter play was also written, or rather worked-over, by Shakspere about 1604. The phrase:

> *"if our virtues Did not go forth of us, 'twere all the same As if we had them not,"*

is developed in the speech of Ulysses to Achilles 96:

> *"A strange fellow here Writes me that man — how dearly ever parted How much in having, or without, or in — Cannot make boast to have that which he hath, Nor feels not what he knows, but by reflection; As when his virtues shining upon others Heat them, and they retort their heat again To the first giver."*

I do not remember in Montaigne any such development of the idea as Shakspere here gives it; indeed, we have seen him putting forth a contrary teaching; and looking to the context, where Ulysses admits the thesis to be "familiar," we are bound to infer a direct source for it. In all probability it derives from Seneca, who in his treatise De Beneficiis 97 throws out the germ 63 of the ideas as to Nature demanding back her gifts, and as to virtue being nothing if not reflected; and even suggests the principle of "thanks and use." 98 This treatise, too, lay to Shakspere's hand in the translation of 1578, where the passages: "Rerum natura nihil dicitur perdere, quia quidquid illi avellitur, ad illam redit; nec perire quidquam potest, quod quo excidat non habet, sed eodem evolvitur unde discedit"; and "quaedam quum sint honesta, pulcherrima summae virtutis, nisi cum altero non habent locum," are translated:

"The nature of a thing cannot be said to have foregone aught, because that whatsoever is plucked from it returneth to it again; neither can anything be lost which hath not whereout of to pass, but windeth back again unto whence it came;"

and

"Some things though they be honest, very goodly and right excellently vertuous, yet have they not their effect but in a co-partner."

Whether it was Shakspere's reading of Montaigne that sent him to Seneca, to whom Montaigne 99 avows so much indebtedness, we of course cannot tell; but it is enough for the purpose of our argument to say that we have 64 here another point or stage in a line of analytical thought on which Shakspere was embarked about 1603, and of which the starting point or initial stimulus was the perusal of Florio's Montaigne. We have the point of contact with Montaigne in Hamlet, where the saying that reason is implanted in us to be used, is seen to be one of the many correspondences of thought between the play and the Essays. The idea is more subtly and deeply developed in Measure for Measure, and still more subtly and philosophically in Troilus and Cressida. The fact of the process of development is all that is here affirmed, over and above the actual phenomena of reproduction before set forth.

As to these, the proposition is that in sum they constitute such an amount of reproduction of Montaigne as explains Jonson's phrase about habitual "stealings." There is no justification for applying that to the passage in the Tempest, since not only is that play not known to have existed in its present form in 1605, 100 when Vol 65 pone was produced, but the phrase plainly alleges not one but many borrowings. I am not aware that extracts from Montaigne have been traced in any others of the English contemporary dramatists. But here in two plays of Shakspere, then fresh in memory — the Second Quarto having been published in 1604 and Measure for Measure produced in the same year — were echoes enough from Montaigne to be noted by Jonson, whom we know to have owned, as did Shakspere, the Florio folio, and to have been Florio's warm admirer. And there seems to be a confirmation of our thesis in the fact that, while we find detached passages savouring of Montaigne in some later plays of the same period, as in one of the concluding period, the Tempest, we do not again find in any one play such a cluster of reminiscences as we have seen in Hamlet and Measure for Measure, though the spirit of Montaigne's thought, turned to a deepening pessimism, may be said to tinge all the later tragedies.

(a) In Othello (? 1604) we have Iago's "'tis in ourselves that we are thus or thus," already considered, to say nothing of Othello's phrase 66 —

> *"I saw it not, thought it not, it harmed not me.... He that is robb'd, not wanting what is stolen, Let him not know it, and he's not robb'd at all."*

— a philosophical commonplace which compares with various passages in the Fortieth Essay.

(b) In Lear (1606) we have such a touch as the king's lines 101 —

> *"And take upon's the mystery of things As if we were God's spies;"*

— which recalls the vigorous protest of the essays, that a man ought soberly to meddle with the judging of the divine laws, 102 where Montaigne avows that if he dared he would put in the category of imposters the

"interpreters and ordinary controllers of the designs of God, setting about to find the causes of each accident, and to see in the secrets of the divine will the incomprehensible motives of its works."

This, again, is a recurrent note with Montaigne; and much of the argument of the Apology is typified in the sentence: —

"What greater vanity can there be than to go about by our proportions and conjectures to guess at God?"

(c) But there is a yet more striking coincidence between a passage in the essay 103 of Judg 67 ing of Others' Death and the speech of Edmund 104

on the subject of stellar influences. In the essay Montaigne sharply derides the habit of ascribing human occurrences to the interference of the stars — which very superstition he was later to support by his own authority in the Apology, as we have seen above, in the passage on the "power and domination" of the celestial bodies. The passage in the thirteenth essay is the more notable in itself, being likewise a protest against human self-sufficiency, though the bearing of the illustration is directly reversed. Here he derides man's conceit: "We entertain and carry all with us: whence it followeth that we deem our death to be some great matter, and which passeth not so easily, nor without a solemn consultation of the stars." Then follow references to C泡r's sayings as to his star, and the "common foppery" as to the sun mourning his death a year.

"And a thousand such, wherewith the world suffers itself to be so easily cony-catched, deeming that our own interests disturb heaven, and his infinity is moved at our least actions. 'There is no such society between 68 heaven and us that by our destiny the shining of the stars should be as mortal as we are.'"

There seems to be an unmistakable reminiscence of this passage in Edmund's speech, where the word "foppery" is a special clue:

"This is the excellent foppery of the world! that when we are sick in fortune (often the surfeit of our own behaviour), we make guilty of our disasters the sun, the moon, and the stars: as if we were villains by necessity; fools by heavenly compulsion; knaves, thieves, and traitors by spherical predominance; drunkards, liars, and adulterers by an enforced obedience of planetary influence; and all that we are evil in, by divine thrusting on...."

(d) Again, in Macbeth (1606), the words of Malcolm to Macduff 105:

> "Give sorrow words: the grief that does not speak, Whispers the
> o'erfraught heart and bids it break"

— an idea which also underlies Macbeth's "this perilous stuff, which weighs upon the heart" — recalls the essay 106 Of Sadness, in which Montaigne remarks on the

"mournful silent stupidity which so doth pierce us when accidents surpassing our strength overwhelm us," and on the way in which "the soul, bursting afterwards forth into tears and complaints ... seemeth to clear and dilate itself"; going on to tell how the German 69 Lord Raisciac looked on *his dead son "till the vehemency of his sad sorrow, having suppressed and choked his vital spirits, felled him stark dead to the ground."*

The parallel here, such as it is, is at least much more vivid than that drawn between Shakspere's lines and one of Seneca:

Curae leves loquuntur: ingentes stupent 107 – "Light troubles speak: the great ones are dumb."

Certainly no one of these latter passages would singly suffice to prove that Shakspere had read Montaigne, though the peculiar coincidence of one word in Edgar's speech with a word in Florio, above noted, would alone raise the question. But even had Shakspere not passed, as we shall see cause to acknowledge, beyond the most melancholy mood of Montaigne into one of far sterner and more stringent pessimism, an absence or infrequency of suggestions of Montaigne in the plays between 1605 and 1610 would be a very natural result of Jonson's gibe in Volpone. That gibe, indeed, is not really so ill-natured as the term "steal" is apt to make it sound for our ears, especially if we are prepossessed – as even Mr. Fleay still seems to be 70 – by the old commentators' notion of a deep ill-will on Jonson's part towards Shakspere. There was probably no such ill-will in the matter, the burly scholar's habit of robust banter being enough to account for the form of his remark. As a matter of fact, his own plays are strewn with classic transcriptions; and though he evidently plumed himself on his power of "invention" 108 in the matter of plots – a faculty which he knew Shakspere to lack – he cannot conceivably have meant to charge his rival with having committed any discreditable plagiarism in drawing upon Montaigne. At most he would mean to convey that borrowing from the English translation of Montaigne was an easy game as compared with his own scholar-like practice of translating from the Greek and Latin, and from out-of-the-way authors, too.

However that might be, the fact stands that Shakspere did about 1604 reproduce Montaigne as we have seen; and it remains to consider what the reproduction signifies, as regards Shakspere's mental development.

71

III.

But first there has to be asked the question whether the Montaigne influence is unique or exceptional. Of the many literary influences which an Elizabethan dramatist might undergo, was Montaigne's the only one which wrought deeply upon Shakspere's spirit, apart from those of his contemporary dramatists and the pre-existing plays, which were then models and points of departure? It is clear that Shakspere must have thought much and critically of the methods and the utterance of his co-rivals in literary art, as he did of the methods of his fellow-actors. The author of the advice to the players in Hamlet was hardly less a critic than a poet; and the sonnet 110 which speaks of its author as

"Desiring this man's art and that man's scope,"

is one of the least uncertain revelations that these enigmatic poems yield us. We may confidently decide, too, with Professor Minto, 109 that the Eighty-sixth Sonnet, beginning:

72

"Was it the full, proud sail of his great verse?"

has reference to Chapman, in whom Shakspere might well see one of his most formidable competitors in poetry. But we are here concerned with influences of thought, as distinct from influences of artistic example; and the question is: Do the plays show any other culture-contact comparable to that which we have been led to recognise in the case of Montaigne's Essays?

The matter cannot be said to have been very fully investigated when even the Montaigne influence has been thus far left so much in the vague. As regards the plots, there has been exhaustive and instructive research during two centuries; and of collations of parallel passages, apart from Montaigne, there has been no lack; but the deeper problem of the dramatist's mental history can hardly be said to have arisen till our own generation. As regards many of the parallel passages, the ground has been pretty well cleared by the dispassionate scholarship brought to bear on them from Farmer onwards; though the idolatry of the Coleridgean school, as represented by Knight, did much to retard scientific conclusions on this as on other points. 73

Farmer's Essay on the Learning of Shakspere (1767) proved for all open-minded readers that much of Shakspere's supposed classical knowledge was derived from translations alone; 111 and further investigation does but establish his general view. 112 Such is the effect of M. Stapfer's chapter on Shakspere's Classical Knowledge; 113 and the pervading argument of that chapter will be found to hold good as against the view suggested, with judicious diffidence, by Dr. John W. Cunliffe, concerning the influence of Seneca's tragedies on Shakspere's. Unquestionably the body of Senecan tragedy, as Dr. Cunliffe's valuable research has shown, did much to colour the style and thought of the Elizabethan drama, as 74 well as to suggest its themes and shape its technique. But it is noteworthy that while there are in the plays, as we have seen, apparent echoes from the Senecan treatises, and while, as we have seen, Dr. Cunliffe suggests sources for some Shaksperean passages in the Senecan tragedies, he is doubtful as to whether they represent any direct study of Seneca by Shakspere.

"Whether Shakspere was directly indebted to Seneca," he writes, "is a question as difficult as it is interesting. As English tragedy advances, there grows up an accumulation of Senecan influence within the English drama, in addition to the original source, and it becomes increasingly difficult to distinguish between the direct and the indirect influence of Seneca. In no case is the difficulty greater than in that of Shakspere. Of Marlowe, Jonson, Chapman, Marston, and Massinger, we can say with certainty that they read Seneca, and reproduced their readings in their tragedies; of Middleton and Heywood we can say with almost equal certainty that they give no sign of direct indebtedness to Seneca; and that they probably came only under the indirect influence, through the imitations of their predecessors and contemporaries. In the case of Shakspere we cannot be absolutely certain either way. Professor Baynes thinks it is probable that Shakspere read Seneca at school; and even if he did not, we may be sure that, at some period of his career, he would 75 turn to the generally accepted model of classical tragedy, either in the original or in the translation." 114

This seems partially inconsistent; and, so far as the evidence from particular parallels goes, we are not led to take with any confidence the view put in the last sentence. The above-noted parallels between Seneca's tragedies and Shakspere's are but cases of citation of sentences likely to have grown proverbial; and the most notable of the others that have been cited by Dr. Cunliffe is one which, as he notes, points to Ychylus as well as to Seneca. The cry of Macbeth:

> *"Will all great Neptune's ocean wash this blood Clean from my hand? No, this my hand will rather The multitudinous seas incarnadine, Making the green one red:"*

certainly corresponds closely with that of Seneca's Hercules: 115

"Quis Tanais, aut quis Nilus, aut quis persica Violentus unda Ti-
gris, aut Rhenus ferox Tagusve ibera turbidus gaza fluens, Abluere
dextram poterit? Arctoum licet Mæotis in me gelida transfundat
mare, Et tota Tethys per meas currat manus, Haerebit altum fac-
inus"

76

and that of Seneca's Hippolytus: 116

"Quis eluet me Tanais? Aut quae barbaris, Mæotis undis pontico
incumbens mari. Non ipso toto magnus Oceano pater Tantum ex-
piarit sceleris."

But these declamations, deriving as they do, to begin with, from Ychylus, 117 are seen from their very recurrence in Seneca to have become stock
speeches for the ancient tragic drama; and they were clearly well-fitted to
become so for the mediæval. The phrases used were already classic when
Catullus employed them before Seneca:

"Suscipit, O Gelli, quantum non ultima Thetys Non genitor Nym-
pharum, abluit Oceanus." 118

In the Renaissance we find the theme reproduced by Tasso; 119 and it
had doubtless been freely used by Shakspere's English predecessors and
contemporaries. What he did was but to set the familiar theme to a rhetoric
whose superb sonority must have left theirs tame, as it leaves Seneca's
stilted in comparison. Marston did his best with it, in a play which may 77
have been written before, though published after, Macbeth 120: —

"Although the waves of all the Northern sea Should flow for ever
through those guilty hands, Yet the sanguinolent stain would ex-
tant be"

— a sad foil to Shakspere's

"The multitudinous seas incarnadine."

It is very clear, then, that we are not here entitled to suppose Shakspere a reader of the Senecan tragedies; and even were it otherwise, the passage in question is a figure of speech rather than a reflection on life or a stimulus to such reflection. And the same holds good of the other interesting but inconclusive parallels drawn by Dr. Cunliffe. Shakspere's

"Diseases desperate grown By desperate appliance are relieved, Or not at all," 121

which he compares with Seneca's

"Et ferrum et ignis s氣 medicin柚oco est. Extrema primo nemo tentavit loco," 122

—a passage that may very well be the original for the modern oracle about fire and iron—is really much closer to the aphorism of Hippocra 78 tes, that "Extreme remedies are proper for extreme diseases," and cannot be said to be more than a proverb. In any case, it lay to Shakspere's hand in Montaigne, 123 as translated by Florio:

"To extreme sicknesses, extreme remedies."

Equally inconclusive is the equally close parallel between Macbeth's

"Canst thou not minister to a mind diseased?"

and the sentence of Hercules:

"Nemo polluto queat Animo mederi." 124

Such a reflection was sure to secure a proverbial vogue, and in The Two Noble Kinsmen (in which Shakspere indeed seems to have had a hand), we have the doctor protesting: "I think she has a perturbed mind, which I cannot minister to." 125

And so, again, with the notable resemblance between Hercules' cry:

"Cur animam in ista luce detineam amplius, Morerque, nihil est. Cuncta jam amisi bona, Mentem, arma, famem, conjugam, natos, manus, Etiam furorem." 126

79

and Macbeth's:

"I have lived long enough: my way of life Is fallen into the sear, the yellow leaf; And that which should accompany old age, As honour, love, obedience, troops of friends, I must not look to have." 127

Here there is indeed every appearance of imitation; but, though the versification in Macbeth's speech is certainly Shakspere's, such a lament had doubtless been made in other English plays, in direct reproduction of Seneca; and Shakspere, in all probability, was again only perfecting some previous declamation.

There is a quite proverbial quality, finally, in such phrases as:

"Things at the worst will cease, or else climb upward To that they were before;" 128

and

"We but teach Bloody instructions, which, being taught, return To plague the inventor." 129

— which might be traced to other sources nearer Shakspere's hand than Seneca. And beyond such sentences and such tropes as those above considered, there was really little or nothing in 80 the tragedies of Seneca to catch Shakspere's eye or ear; nothing to generate in him a deep philosophy of life or to move him to the manifold play of reflection which gives his later tragedies their commanding intellectuality. Some such stimulus, as we have seen, he might indeed have drawn from one or two of Seneca's treatises, which do, in their desperately industrious manner, cover a good deal of intellectual ground, making some tolerable discoveries by the way. But by the tests alike of quantity and quality of reproduced matter, it is clear that

the indirect influence of the Senecan tragedies and treatises on Shakspere was slight compared with the direct influence of Montaigne's essays. Nor is it hard to see why; even supposing Shakspere to have had Seneca at hand in translation. Despite Montaigne's own leaning to Seneca, as compared with Cicero, we may often say of the former what Montaigne says of the latter, that "his manner of writing seemeth very tedious." Over the De Beneficiis and the De Ira one is sometimes moved to say, as the essayist does 130 over Cicero, "I understand sufficiently what death 81 and voluptuousness are; let not a man busy himself to anatomise them." For the swift and penetrating flash of Montaigne, which either goes to the heart of a matter once for all or opens up a far vista of feeling and speculation, leaving us newly related to our environment and even to our experience, Seneca can but give us a conscientious examination of the ground, foot by foot, with a policeman's lantern, leaving us consciously footsore, eyesore, and ready for bed. Under no stress of satisfaction from his best finds can we be moved to call him a man of genius, which is just what we call Montaigne after a few pages. It is the broad difference between industry and inspiration, between fecundity and pregnancy, between Jonson and Shakspere. And, though a man of genius is not necessarily dependent on other men of genius for stimulus, we shall on scrutiny find reason to believe that in Shakspere's case the nature of the stimulus counted for a great deal.

Even before that is made clear, however, there can be little hesitation about dismissing the only other outstanding theory of a special intellectual influence undergone by Shakspere—the 82 theory of Dr. Benno Tschischwitz, that he read and was impressed by the Italian writings of Giordano Bruno. In this case, the bases of the hypothesis are of the scantiest and the flimsiest. Bruno was in England from 1583 to 1586, before Shakspere came to London. Among his patrons were Sidney and Leicester, but neither Southampton nor Pembroke. In all his writings only one passage can be cited which even faintly suggests a coincidence with any in Shakspere; and in that the suggestion is faint indeed. In Bruno's ill-famed comedy Il Candelajo, Octavio asks the pedant Manfurio, "Che e la materia di vostri versi," and the pedant replies, "Litter太syllab太dictio et oratio, partes propinqu染t remot欢 on which Octavio again asks: "Io dico, quale e il suggetto et il proposito." 131 So far as it goes this is something of a parallel to Polonius's question to Hamlet as to what he reads, and Hamlet's answer, "Words, words." But the scene is obviously a stock situation; and if there are any passages in Hamlet which clearly belong to the pre-Shaksperean play, the fooling of Hamlet 83 with Polonius is one of them.

And beyond this, Dr. Tschischwitz's parallels are flatly unconvincing, or rather they promptly put themselves out of court. He admits that nothing else in Bruno's comedy recalls anything else in Shakspere; 132 but he goes on to find analogies between other passages in Hamlet and some of Bruno's philosophic doctrines. Quoting Bruno's theorem that all things are made up of indestructible atoms, and that death is but a transformation, Dr. Tschischwitz cites as a reproduction of it Hamlet's soliloquy:

"O, that this too, too solid flesh would melt!"

It is difficult to be serious over such a contention; and it is quite impossible for anybody out of Germany or the Bacon-Shakspere party to be as serious over it as Dr. Tschischwitz, who finds that Hamlet's figure of the melting of flesh into dew is an illustration of Bruno's "atomic system," and goes on to find a further Brunonian significance in Hamlet's jeering answers to the king's demand for the body of Polonius. Of 84 these passages he finds the source or suggestion in one which he translates from Bruno's Cena de le Ceneri: –

"For to this matter, of which our planet is formed, death and dissolution do not come; and the annihilation of all nature is not possible; but it attains from time to time, by a fixed law, to renew itself and to change all its parts, rearranging and recombining them; all this necessarily taking place in a determinate series, under which everything assumes the place of another." 133

In the judgment of Dr. Tschischwitz, this theorem, which anticipates so remarkably the modern scientific conception of the universe, "elucidates" Hamlet's talk about worms and bodies, and his further sketch of the progress of Alexander's dust to the plugging of a beer-barrel. It seems unnecessary to argue that all this is the idlest supererogation. The passages cited from Hamlet, all of them found in the First Quarto, might have been drafted by a much lesser man than Shakspere, and that without ever having heard of Bruno or the theory of the indestructibility of matter. There is nothing in the case approaching to a reproduction of Bruno's far-reaching thought; while 85 on the contrary the "leave not a wrack behind," in the Tempest, is an expression which sets aside, as if it were unknown, the conception of an endless transmutation of matter, in a context where the thought would naturally suggest itself to one who had met with it. Where Hamlet is merely sardonic in the plane of popular or at least exoteric humour, Dr. Tschischwitz credits him with pantheistic philosophy. Where, on the other hand, Hamlet speaks feelingly and ethically of the serious side of drunkenness, 134 Dr. Tschischwitz parallels the speech with a sentence in the Bestia Trionfante, which gives a merely Rabelaisian picture of drunken practices. 135 Yet again, he puts Bruno's large aphorism, "Sol et homo generant hominem," beside Hamlet's gibe about the sun breeding maggots in a dead dog — a phrase possible to any euphuist of the period. That the parallels amount at best to little, Dr. Tschischwitz himself indirectly admits, though he proceeds to a new extravagance of affirmation:

"We do not maintain that such expressions are philosophemes, or that Shakspere otherwise went any 86 deeper into Bruno's system than suited his purpose, but that such passages show Shakspere, at the time of his writing of Hamlet, to have already reached the heights of the thought of the age (Zeitbewusstsein), and to have made himself familiar with the most abstract of the sciences. Many hitherto almost unintelligible passages in Hamlet are now cleared up by the poet's acquaintance with the atomic philosophy and the writings of the Nolan."

All this belongs to the uncritical method of the German Shakspere-criticism of the days before Rmelin. It is quite possible that Shakspere may have heard something of Bruno's theories from his friends; and we may be sure that much of Bruno's teaching would have profoundly interested him. If Bruno's lectures at Oxford on the immortality of the soul included the matter he published later on the subject, they may have called English attention to the Pythagorean lore concerning the fate of the soul after death, 136 above cited from Montaigne. We might again, on Dr. Tschischwitz's lines, trace the verses on the "shaping fantasies" of "the lunatic, the lover, and the poet," in the Midsummer Night's Dream, 137 to such a passage in Bruno as this:—

87

"The first and most capital painter is the vivacity of the phantasy; the first and most capital poet is the inspiration that originally arises with the impulse of deep thought, or is set up by that, through the divine or akin-to-divine breath of which they feel themselves moved to the fit expression of their thoughts. For each it creates the other principle. Therefore are the philosophers in a certain sense painters; the poets, painters and philosophers; the painters, philosophers and poets: true poets, painters, and philosophers love and reciprocally admire each other. There is no philosopher who does not poetise and paint. Therefore is it said, not without reason: To

understand is to perceive the figures of phantasy, and understanding is phantasy, or is nothing without it." 138

But since Shakspere does not recognisably echo a passage which he would have been extremely likely to produce in such a context, had he known it, we are bound to decide that he had not even heard it cited, much less read it. And so with any other remote resemblances between his work and that of any author whom he may have read. In regard even to passages in Shakspere which come much nearer their originals than any of these above cited come to Bruno, we are forced to decide that Shakspere got his thought at second or third hand. Thus 88 the famous passage in Henry V., 139 in which the Archbishop figures the State as a divinely framed harmony of differing functions, is clearly traceable to Plato's Republic and Cicero's De Republica; yet rational criticism must decide with M. Stapfer 140 that Shakspere knew neither of these treatises, but got his suggestion from some English translation or citation.

In fine, we are constrained by all our knowledge concerning Shakspere, as well as by the abstract principles of proof, to regard him in general as a reader of his own language only, albeit not without a smattering of others; and among the books in his own language which we know him to have read in, and can prove him to have been influenced by, we come back to Montaigne's Essays, as by far the most important and the most potential for suggestion and provocation.

89

IV.

To have any clear idea, however, of what Montaigne did or could do for Shakspere, we must revise our conception of the poet in the light of the positive facts of his life and circumstances – a thing made difficult for us in England through the transcendental direction given to our Shakspere lore by those who first shaped it sympathetically, to wit, Coleridge and the Germans. An adoring idea of Shakspere, as a mind of unapproachable superiority, has thus become so habitual with most of us that it is difficult to reduce our notion to terms of normal individuality, of character and mind as we know them in life. When we read Coleridge, Schlegel, and Gervinus, or even the admirable essay of Charles Lamb, or the eloquent appreciations of Mr. Swinburne, or such eulogists as Hazlitt and Knight, we are in a world of abstract Æsthetics or of abstract ethics; we are not within sight of the man Shakspere, who became an actor for a 90 livelihood in an age when the best actors played in inn-yards for rude audiences, mostly illiterate and not a little brutal; then added to his craft of acting the craft of play-patching and refashioning; who had his partnership share of the pence and sixpences paid by the mob of noisy London prentices and journeymen and idlers that filled the booth theatre in which his company performed; who sued his debtors rigorously when they did not settle-up; worked up old plays or took a hand in new, according as the needs of his concern and his fellow-actors dictated; and finally went with his carefully collected fortune to spend his last years in ease and quiet in the country town in which he was born. Our sympathetic critics, even when, like Dr. Furnivall, they know absolutely all the archæological facts as to theatrical life in Shakspere's time, do not seem to bring those facts into vital touch with their æsthetic estimate of his product; they remain under the spell of Coleridge and Gervinus. 141 Emerson, it is true, 91 protested at the close of his essay that he "could not marry this fact," of Shakspere's being a jovial actor and manager, "to his verse;" but that deliverance has served only as a text for those who have embraced the fantastic tenet that Shakspere was but the theatrical agent and representative of Bacon; a delusion of which the vogue may be partly traced to the lack of psychological solidity in the ordinary presentment of Shakspere by his admirers. The heresy, of course, merely leaps over the difficulty, into 92 absolute irrelevance. Emerson was intellectually to blame in that, seeing as he did the hiatus between the poet's life and the prevailing conception of his verse, he did not try to conceive it all anew, but rather resigned himself to the solution that Shakspere's mind was out of human ken. "A good reader can in a sort nestle into Plato's brain and think from thence," he said; "but not into Shakspere's; we are still out of doors." We should indeed remain so for ever did we not set about patiently picking the locks where the transcendentalist has dreamily turned away.

It is imperative that we should recommence vigilantly with the concrete facts, ignoring all the merely æsthetic and metaphysic syntheses. Where Coleridge and Schlegel more or less ingeniously invite us to acknowledge a miraculous artistic perfection, where Lamb more movingly gives forth the intense vibration aroused in his spirit by Shakspere's ripest work, we must turn back to track down the youth from Stratford; son of a burgess once prosperous, but destined to sink steadily in the world; married at eighteen, under pressure of circumstances, 93 with small prospect of income, to the woman of twenty-five; ill at ease in that position; and at length, having made friends with a travelling company of actors, come to London to earn a *living in any tolerable way by means of his moderate education, his "small Latin and less Greek," his knack of fluent rhyming, and his turn for play-acting. To know him as he began we must measure him narrowly by his first performances. These are not to be looked for in even the earliest of his plays, not one of which can be taken to represent his young and unaided faculty, whether as regards construction or diction. Collaboration, the natural resort of the modern dramatist, must have been to some extent forced on him in those years by the nature of his situation; and after all that has been said by adorers of the quality of his wit and his verse in such early comedies as Love's Labour Lost and The Two Gentlemen of Verona, the critical reader is apt to be left pretty evenly balanced between the two reflections that the wit and the versification have indeed at times a certain happy naturalness of their own, and that nevertheless, if they really 94 be Shakspere's throughout, the most remarkable thing in the matter is his later progress. But even apart from such disputable issues, we may safely say with Mr. Fleay that "there is not a play of his that can be referred even on the rashest conjecture to a date anterior to 1594, which does not bear the plainest internal evidence of having been refashioned at a later time." 142 These plays, then, with all their evidences of immaturity, of what Mr. Bagehot called "clever young-mannishness," cannot serve us as safe measures of Shakspere's mind at the beginning of his career.*

But it happens that we have such a measure in performances which, since they imply no technical arrangement, are of a homogenous literary substance, and can be shown to be the work of a man brought up in the Warwickshire dialect, 143 are not even challenged, I believe, by the adherents of the Baconian faith. The tasks which the greatest of our poets set himself when near the age of thirty, and to which he presumably brought all the powers of which he was then 95 conscious, were the uninspired and pitilessly prolix poems of Venus and Adonis and The Rape of Lucrece, the first consisting of some 1,200 lines and the second of more than 1,800; one a calculated picture of female concupiscence and the other a still more calculated picture of female chastity: the two alike abnormally fluent, yet external, unimpassioned, endlessly descriptive, elaborately unimpressive. Save for the sexual attraction of the subjects, on the commercial side of which the poet had obviously reckoned in choosing them, these performances could have no unstudious readers in our day and few warm admirers in their own, so little sign do they give of any high poetic faculty save the two which singly go so often without any determining superiority of mind — inexhaustible flow of words and endless observation of concrete detail. Of

the countless thrilling felicities of phrase and feeling for which Shakspere is
renowned above all English poets, not one, I think, is to be found in those
three thousand fluently-scanned and smoothly-worded lines: on the contrary, the wearisome succession of stanzas, stretching the succinct themes 96
immeasurably beyond all natural fitness and all narrative interest, might
seem to signalise such a lack of artistic judgment as must preclude all great
performance; while the apparent plan of producing an effect by mere mul-
tiplication of words, mere extension of description without intension of
idea, might seem to prove a lack of capacity for any real depth of passion.
They were simply manufactured poems, consciously constructed for the
market, the first designed at the same time to secure the patronage of the
Mæcenas of the hour, Lord Southampton, to whom it was dedicated, and the
second produced and similarly dedicated on the strength of the success of
the first. The point here to be noted is that they gained the poet's ends.
They succeeded as saleable literature, and they gained the Earl's favour.

And the rest of the poet's literary career, from this point forward, seems
to have been no less prudently calculated. Having plenty of evidence that
men could not make a living by poetry, even if they produced it with facility; and that they could as little count on living steadily by the sale of plays,
he joined with his 97 trade of actor the business not merely of playwright
but of part-sharer in the takings of the theatre. The presumption from all
we know of the commercial side of the play-making of the times is that, for
whatever pieces Shakspere touched up, collaborated in, or composed for his
company, he received a certain payment once for all; 144 since there was no
reason why his partners should treat his plays differently in this regard
from the plays they bought of other men. Doubtless, when his reputation
was made, the payments would be considerable. But the main source of his
income, or rather of the accumulations with which he bought land and
house and tithes at Stratford, must have been his share in the takings of the
theatre — a share which would doubtless increase as the earlier partners
disappeared. He must have speedily become the principal man in the firm,
combining as he did the work of composer, reviser, and adaptor of plays
with that of actor and working partner. We are thus dealing with a temperament or mentality not at all obviously original or 98 masterly, not at
all conspicuous at the outset for intellectual depth or seriousness, not at all
obtrusive of its "mission;" but exhibiting simply a gift for acting, an abundant faculty of rhythmical speech, and a power of minute observation,
joined with a thoroughly practical or commercial handling of the problem
of life, in a calling not usually taken-to by commercially-minded men.

What emerges for us thus far is the conception of a very plastic intelligence, a good deal led and swayed by immediate circumstances; but at bottom very sanely related to life, and so possessing a latent faculty for controlling its destinies; not much cultured, not profound, not deeply passionate; not particularly reflective though copious in utterance; a personality which of itself, if under no pressure of pecuniary need, would not be likely to give the world any serious sign of mental capacity whatever.

In order, then, that such a man as this should develop into the Shakspere of the great tragedies and tragic comedies, there must concur two kinds of life-conditions with those already noted — the fresh conditions of deeply-moving experience and of deep intellectual stimulus. Without 99 these, such a mind would no more arrive at the highest poetic and dramatic capacity than, lacking the spur of necessity or of some outside call, it would be moved to seek poetic and dramatic utterance for its own relief. There is no sign here of an innate burden of thought, bound to be delivered; there is only the sensitive plate or responsive faculty, capable of giving back with peculiar vividness and spontaneity every sort of impression which may be made on it. The faculty, in short, which could produce those 3,000 fluent lines on the bare data of the stories of Venus and Adonis and Tarquin and Lucrece, with only the intellectual material of a rakish Stratford lad's schooling and reading, and the culture coming of a few years' association with the primitive English stage and its hangers-on, was capable of broadening and deepening, with vital experience and vital culture, into the poet of Lear and Macbeth. But the vital culture must come to it, like the experience: this was not a man who would go out of his way to seek the culture. A man so minded, a man who would bear hardship in order to win knowledge, would not have settled down so easily into the 100 actor-manager with a good share in the company's profits. There is almost nothing to show that the young Shakspere read anything save current plays, tales, and poems. Such a notable book as North's Plutarch, published in 1579, does not seem to have affected his literary activity till about the year 1600: and even then the subject of Julius Cæsar may have been suggested to him by some other play-maker, as was the case with his chronicle histories. In his contemporary, Ben Jonson, we do have the type of the young man bent on getting scholarship as the best thing possible to him. The bricklayer's apprentice, unwillingly following the craft of his stepfather, sticking obstinately all the while to his Horace and his Homer, resolute to keep and to add to the humanities he had learned in the grammar school, stands out clearly alongside of the other, far less enthusiastic for knowledge and let-

ters, but also far more plastically framed, and at the same time far more clearly alive to the seriousness of the struggle for existence as a matter of securing the daily bread-and-butter. It may be, indeed—who knows—that but for that peculiarly early 101 marriage, with its consequent family responsibilities, Shakspere would have allowed himself a little more of youthful breathing-time: it may be that it was the existence of Ann Hathaway and her three children that made him a seeker for pelf rather than a seeker for knowledge in the years between twenty and thirty, when the concern for pelf sits lightly on most intellectual men. The thesis undertaken in Love's Labour Lost—that the truly effective culture is that of life in the world rather than that of secluded study—perhaps expresses a process of inward and other debate in which the wish has become father to the thought. Scowled upon by jealous collegians like Greene for presuming, actor as he was, to write dramas, he must have asked himself whether there was not something to be gained from such schooling as theirs. 145 But then he certainly made more than was needed to keep the Stratford household going; and the clear shallow flood of Venus and Adonis and the Rape of Lucrece stands for ever to show how far from tragic consciousness was the young 102 husband and father when close upon thirty years old. It was in 1596 that his little Hamnet died at Stratford; and there is nothing to show, says Mr. Fleay, 146 that Shakspere had ever been there in the interval between his departure in 1587 and the child's funeral.

But already, it may be, some vital experience had come. Whatever view we take of the drama of the sonnets, we may so far adopt Mr. Fleay's remarkable theory 147 as to surmise that the central episode of faithless love occurred about 1594. If so, here was enough to deepen and impassion the plastic personality of the rhymer of Venus and Adonis; to add a new string to the heretofore Mercurial lyre. All the while, too, he was undergoing the kind of culture and of psychological training involved in his craft of acting—a culture involving a good deal of contact with the imaginative literature of the Renaissance, so far as then translated, and a psychological training of great though little recognised importance to the dramatist. It seems 103 obvious that the practice of acting, by a plastic and receptive temperament, capable of manifold appreciation, must have counted for much in developing the faculties at once of sympathy and expression. In this respect Shakspere stood apart from his rivals, with their merely literary training. And in point of fact, we do find in his plays, year by year, a strengthening sense of the realities of human nature, despite their frequently idealistic method of portraiture, the verbalism and factitiousness of much of their wit, and their conventionality of plot. Above all things, the man who drew so many fancifully delightful types of womanhood must have been intensely appreciative of the charm of sex; and it is on that side that we are to look for his first contacts with the deeper forces of life. What marks off the Shakspere of thirty-five, in fine, from all his rivals, is just his peculiarly true and new 148 expression of the living grace of womanhood, always, it is true, abstracted to the form of poetry and skilfully purified from the blemishes of the actual, but none the less con 104 vincing and stimulating. We are here in presence at once of a rare receptive faculty and a rare expressive faculty: the plastic organism of the first poems touched through and through with a hundred vibrations of deeper experience; the external and extensive method gradually ripening into an internal and intensive; the innate facility of phrase and alertness of attention turned from the physical to the psychical. But still it is to the psychics of sex, for the most part, that we are limited. Of the deeps of human nature, male nature, as apart from the love of woman, the playwright still shows no special perception, save in the vivid portrait of Shylock, the exasperated Jew. The figures in which we can easily recognise his hand in the earlier historical plays are indeed marked by his prevailing sanity of perception; always they show the play of the seeing eye, the ruling sense of reality which shaped his life; it is this visible actuality that best marks them off from the non-Shaksperean figures around them. And in the wonderful figures of Falstaff and his group we have a roundness of comic reality to which nothing else in modern literature thus 105 far could be compared. But still this, the most remarkable of all, remains comic reality; and, what is more, it is a comic reality of which, as in the rest of his work, the substratum was pre-Shaksperean. For it is clear that the figure of Falstaff, as Old-castle, had been popularly successful before Shakspere took hold of it: 149 and what he did here, as elsewhere, with his uninventive mind, in which the faculty of imagination always rectified and expanded rather than originated types and actions, was doubtless to give the hues and tones of perfect life to the half-real inventions of others. This must always be insisted on as the special psychological characteristic of Shakspere. Excepting in the doubtful case of Love's Labour Lost, he never invented a plot; his male characters are almost always developments from an already sketched original; it is in drawing his heroines, where he is most idealistic, that he seems to have been most independently creative, his originals here being doubtless the women who had charmed him, set living in ideal scenes to charm others. And it resulted from this specialty of structure 106 that the greater reality of his earlier male historic figures, as compared with those of most of *his rivals, is largely a matter of saner and more felicitous declamation — the play of his great and growing faculty of expression — since he had no more special knowledge of the types in hand than had his competitors. It is only when his unequalled receptive faculty has been acted upon by a peculiarly concentrated and readily assimilated body of culture, the English translation by Sir Thomas North of Amyot's French translation of Plutarch's Lives, that we find Shakspere incontestably superior to his contemporaries in the virile treatment of virile problems no less than in the sympathetic rendering of emotional charm and tenderness and the pathos of passion. The tragedy of Romeo and Juliet, with all its burning fervours and swooning griefs, remains for us a picture of the luxury of woe: it is truly said of it that it is not fundamentally unhappy. But in Julius Cæsar we have touched a further depth of sadness. For the moving tragedy of circumstance, of lovers sundered by fate only to be swiftly joined in exultant death, we have the profounder tragedy 107 of mutually destroying energies, of grievously miscalculating men, of failure and frustration dogging the steps of the strenuous and the wise, of destiny searching out the fatal weakness of the strong. To the poet has now been added the reader; to the master of the pathos of passion the student of the tragedy of universal life. It is thus by culture and experience — culture limited but concentrated, and experience limited but intense — that the man Shakspere has been intelligibly made into the dramatist Shakspere as we find him when he comes to his greatest tasks. For the formation of the supreme artist there was needed alike the purely plastic organism and the special culture to which it was so uniquely fitted to respond; culture that came without search, and could be undergone as spontaneously as the experience of life itself; knowledge that needed no more wooing than Ann Hathaway, or any dubious angel in the sonnets. In the English version of Plutarch's Lives, pressed upon him doubtless by the play-making plans of other men, Shakspere found the most effectively concentrated history of ancient humanity that could possibly have reached him; 108 and he responded to the stimulus with all his energy of expression because he received it so freely and vitally, in respect alike of his own plasticity and the fact that the vehicle of the impression was his mother tongue. It is plain that to the last he made no secondary study of antiquity. He made blunders which alone might warn the Baconians off their vain quest: he had no notion of chronology: finding Cato retrospectively spoken of by Plutarch as one to whose ideal Coriolanus had risen, he makes a comrade of Coriolanus say it, as if Cato were a dead celebrity in Coriolanus' day; just as he makes Hector quote Aristotle in Troy. These clues are not to be put aside with æsthetic platitudes: they are capital items in our knowledge of the man. And if even the idolator feels perturbed by their obtrusion, he has but to reflect that where the trained scholars around Shakspere reproduced antiquity with greater accuracy in minor things, tithing the mint and anise and cumin of erudition, they gave us of the central human forces, which it was their special business to realise, mere hollow and tedious parodies. Jonson was a scholar whose variety 109 of classic reading might have constituted him a specialist to-day; but Jonson's ancients are mostly dead for us, even as are Jonson's moderns, because they are the expression of a psychic faculty which could neither rightly perceive reality, nor rightly express what it did perceive. He represents industry in art without inspiration. The two contrasted pictures, of Jonson writing out his harangues in prose in order to turn them into verse, and of Shakspere giving his lines unblotted to the actors – speaking in verse, in the white heat of his cerebration, as spontaneously as he breathed – these historic data, which happen to be among the most perfectly certified that we possess concerning the two men, give us at once half the secret of one and all the secret of the other. Jonson had the passion for book knowledge, the patience for hard study, the faculty for plot-invention; and withal he produced dramatic work which gives little or no permanent pleasure. Shakspere had none of these characteristics; and yet, being the organism he was, it only needed the culture which fortuitously reached him in his own tongue to make him successively the greatest 110 dramatic master of eloquence, mirth, charm, tenderness, passion, pathos, pessimism, and philosophic serenity that literature can show, recognisably so even though his work be almost constantly hampered by the framework of other men's enterprises, which he was so singularly content to develop or improve. Hence the critical importance of following up the culture which evolved him, and above all, that which finally touched him to his most memorable performance.*

V.

111 It is to Montaigne, then, that we now come, in terms of our preliminary statement of evidence. When Florio's translation was published, in 1603, Shakspere was thirty-seven years old, and he had written or refashioned King John, Henry IV., The Merchant of Venice, A Midsummer Night's Dream, Richard II., Twelfth Night, As You Like It, Henry V., Romeo and Juliet, The Merry Wives of Windsor, and Julius C泡r. It is very likely that he knew Florio, being intimate with Jonson, who was Flo-

rio's friend and admirer; and the translation, long on the stocks, must have been discussed in his hearing. Hence, presumably, his immediate perusal of it. Portions of it he may very well have seen or heard of before it was fully printed (necessarily a long task in the then state of the handicraft); but in the book itself, we have seen abundant reason to believe, he read largely in 1603-4.

Having inductively proved the reading, and at the same time the fact of the impression it [112] made, we may next seek to realise deductively what kind of impression it was fitted to make. We can readily see what North's Plutarch could be and was to the sympathetic and slightly-cultured playwright; it was nothing short of a new world of human knowledge; a living vision of two great civilisations, giving to his universe a vista of illustrious realities beside which the charmed gardens of Renaissance romance and the bustling fields of English chronicle-history were as pleasant dreams or noisy interludes. He had done wonders with the chronicles; but in presence of the long muster-rolls of Greece and Rome he must have felt their insularity; and he never returned to them in the old spirit. But if Plutarch could do so much for him, still greater could be the service rendered by Montaigne. The difference, broadly speaking, is very much as the difference in philosophic reach between Julius Cæsar and Hamlet, between Coriolanus and Lear.

For what was in its nett significance Montaigne's manifold book, coming thus suddenly, in a complete and vigorous translation, into English life and into Shakspere's ken? Simply [113] the most living book then existing in Europe. This is not the place, nor am I the person, to attempt a systematic estimate of the most enduring of French writers, who has stirred to their best efforts the ablest of French critics; but I must needs try to indicate briefly, as I see it, his significance in general European culture. And I would put it that Montaigne is really, for the civilised world at this day, what Petrarch has been too enthusiastically declared to be – the first of the moderns. He is so as against even the great Rabelais, because Rabelais misses directness, misses universality, misses lucidity, in his gigantic mirth; he is so as against Petrarch, because he is emphatically an impressionist where Petrarch is a framer of studied compositions; he is so against Erasmus, because Erasmus also is a framer of artificial compositions in a dead language, where Montaigne writes with absolute spontaneity in a language not only living but growing. Only Chaucer, and he only in the Canterbury Tales, can be thought of as a true modern before Montaigne; and Chaucer is there too English to be significant for all Europe. The high *figure of Dante 114 is decisively medi涨l: it is the central point in medi涨l literature. Montaigne was not only a new literary phenomenon in his own day: he remains so still; for his impressionism, which he carried to such lengths in originating it, is the most modern of literary inspirations; and all our successive literary and artistic developments are either phases of the same inspiration or transient reactions against it. Where literature in the mass has taken centuries to come within sight of the secret that the most intimate form of truth is the most interesting, he went, in his one collection of essays, so far towards absolute self-expression that our practice is still in the rear of his, which is quite too unflinching for contemporary nerves. Our bonne foi is still sophisticated in comparison with that of the great Gascon. Of all essayists who have yet written, he is the most transparent, the most sincere even in his stratagems, the most discursive, the most free-tongued, and therefore the most alive. A classic commonplace becomes in his hands a new intimacy of feeling: where verbal commonplaces have, as it were, glazed over the surface of our sense, he goes behind them to rouse anew the 115 living nerve. And there is no theme on which he does not some time or other dart his sudden and searching glance. It is truly said of him by Emerson that "there have been men with deeper insight; but, one would say, never a man with such abundance of thoughts: he is never dull, never insincere, and has the genius to make the reader care for all that he cares for. Cut these words and they bleed; they are vascular and alive." Such a voice, speaking at Shakspere's ear in an English nearly as racy and nervous as the incomparable old-new French of the original, was in itself a revelation.*

I have said above that we seem to see passing from Montaigne to Shakspere a vibration of style as well as of thought; and it would be difficult to overstate the importance of such an influence. A writer affects us often more by the pulse and pressure of his speech than by his matter. Such an action is indeed the secret of all great literary reputations; and in no author of any age are the cadence of phrases and the beat of words more provocative of attention than in Montaigne. They must have affected Shakspere as they have done so many others; and in 116 point of fact his work, from Hamlet forth, shows a gain in nervous tension and pith, fairly attributable to the stirring impact of the style of Montaigne, with its incessancy of stroke, its opulence of colour, its hardy freshness of figure and epithet, its swift, unflagging stride. Seek in any of Shakspere's plays for such a strenuous rush of idea and rhythm as pulses through the soliloquy:

"How all occasions do inform against me,"

and you will gather that there has been a technical change wrought, no less than a moral and an intellectual. The poet's nerves have caught a new vibration.

But it was not merely a congenial felicity and energy of utterance that Montaigne brought to bear on his English reader, though the more we consider this quality of spontaneity in the essayist the more we shall realise its perennial fascination. The culture-content of Montaigne's book is more than even the self-revelation of an extremely vivacious and reflective intelligence; it is the living quintessence of all Latin criticism of life, and of a large part of Greek; a quintessence as fresh and pungent as the essay 117 ist's expression of his special individuality. For Montaigne stands out among all the humanists of the epochs of the Renaissance and the Reformation in respect of the peculiar directness of his contact with Latin literature. Other men must have come to know Latin as well as he; and hundreds could write it with an accuracy and facility which, if he were ever capable of it, he must, by his own confession, have lost before middle life, 150 though he read it perfectly to the last. But he is the only modern man whom we know to have learned Latin as a mother tongue; and this fact was probably just as important in psychology as was the similar fact, in Shakspere's case, of his whole adult culture being acquired in his own language. It seems to me, at least, that there is something significant in the facts: (1) that the man who most vividly brought the spirit or outcome of classic culture into touch with the general European intelligence, in the age when the modern languages first decisively asserted their birthright, learned his Latin as a living and not as a dead tongue, and knew Greek literature almost 118 solely by translation; (2) that the dramatist who of all of his craft has put most of breathing vitality into his pictures of ancient history, despite endless inaccuracies of detail, read his authorities only in his own language; and (3) that the English poet who in our own century has most intensely and delightedly sympathised with the Greek spirit—I mean Keats—read his Homer only in an English translation. As regards Montaigne, the full importance of the fact does not seem to me to have been appreciated by the critics. Villemain, indeed, who perhaps could best realise it, remarked in his youthful age that the fashion in which the elder Montaigne had his child taught Latin would bring the boy to the reading of the classics with an eager interest where others had been already fatigued by the toil of grammar; but beyond this the peculiarity of the case has not been much considered. Montaigne, however, gives us details which seem full of suggestion to scientific educationists. "Without art, without book, without grammar or precept, without whipping, without tears, I learned a Latin as pure as my master could give;" and his first 119 exercises were to turn bad Latin into good. 151 So he read his Ovid's Metamorphoses at seven or eight, where other forward boys had the native fairy tales; and a wise teacher led him later through Virgil and Terence and Plautus and the Italian poets in the same freedom of spirit. Withal, he never acquired any facility in Greek, 152 and, refusing to play the apprentice where he was accustomed to be master, 153 he declined to construe in a difficult tongue; read his Plutarch in Amyot; and his Plato, doubtless, in the Latin version. It all goes with the peculiar spontaneity of his mind, his reactions, his style; and it was in virtue of this undulled spontaneity that he was fitted to be for Shakspere, as he has since been for so many other great writers, an intellectual stimulus unique in kind and in potency.

This fact of Montaigne's peculiar influence on other spirits, comparatively considered, may make it easier for some to conceive that his influence on Shakspere could be so potent as has been above asserted. Among those whom we know him to have acted upon in the highest 120 degree — setting aside the disputed case of Bacon — are Pascal, Montesquieu, Rousseau, Flaubert, Emerson, and Thoreau. In the case of Pascal, despite his uneasy assumption that his philosophy was contrary to Montaigne's, the influence went so far that the Pensées again and again set forth Pascal's doctrine in passages taken almost literally from the Essays. Stung by the lack of all positive Christian credence in Montaigne, Pascal represents him as "putting all things in doubt;" whereas it is just by first putting all things in doubt that Pascal justifies his own credence. The only difference is that where Montaigne, disparaging the powers of reason by the use of that very reason, used his "doubt" to defend himself alike against the atheists and the orthodox Christians, Catholic or Protestant, himself standing simply to the classic theism of antiquity, Pascal seeks to demolish the theists with the atheists, falling back on the Christian faith after denying the capacity of the human reason to judge for itself. The two procedures were of course alike fallacious; but though Pascal, the more austere thinker of the two, readily saw the invalidity of Mon 121 taigne's as a defence of theism, he could do no more for himself than repeat the process, disparaging reason in the very language of the essayist, and setting up in his turn his private predilection in Montaigne's manner. In sum, his philosophy is just Montaigne's, turned to the needs of a broken spirit instead of a confident one — to the purposes of a chagrined and exhausted convertite instead of a theist of the stately school of Cicero and Seneca and Plutarch. Without Montaigne, one feels, the Pens 伽 might never have been written: they represent to-day, for all vigilant readers, rather the painful struggles of a wounded intelligence to fight down the doubts it has caught from contact with other men's thought than any coherent or durable philosophic construction.

It would be little more difficult to show the debt of the Esprit des Lois to Montaigne's inspiration, even if we had not Montesquieu's avowal that "In most authors I see the man who writes: in Montaigne, the man who thinks." 154 That is precisely Montaigne's significance, in 122 sociology as in philosophy. His whole activity is a seeking for causes; and in the very act of undertaking to "humble reason" he proceeds to instruct and re-edify it by endless corrective comparison of facts. To be sure, he departed so far from his normal bonne foi as to affect to think there could be no certainties while parading a hundred of his own, and with these some which were but pretences; and his pet doctrine of daimonic fortune is not ostensibly favourable to social science; but in the concrete, he is more of a seeker after rational law than any humanist of his day. In discussing sumptuary laws, he anticipates the economics of the eighteenth and nineteenth centuries, as in discussing ecclesiastical law he anticipates the age of tolerance; in discussing criminal law, the work of Beccaria; in discussing ·riori science, the protest of Bacon; and in discussing education, many of the ideas of to-day. And it would be difficult to cite, in humanist literature before our own century, a more comprehensive expression of the idea of natural law than this paragraph of the Apology:

"If nature enclose within the limits of her ordinary 123 progress, as all other things, so the beliefs, the judgments, the opinions of men, if they have their revolutions, their seasons, their birth, and their death, even as cabbages; if heaven doth move, agitate, and roll them at his pleasure, what powerful and permanent authority do we ascribe unto them. If, by uncontrolled experience, we palpably touch [orig. "Si par experience nous touchons ·a main," i.e., nous maintenons, nous pr勤偵ndons: an idiom which Florio has not understood] that the form of our being depends of the air, of the climate, and of the soil wherein we are born, and not only the hair, the stature, the complexion, and the countenance, but also the soul's faculties ... in such manner that as fruits and beasts do spring up diverse and different, so men are born, either more or less war-like, martial, just, temperate, and docile; here subject to wine, there to theft and whoredom, here inclined to superstition, there addicted to misbelieving.... If sometimes we see one art to flourish, or a belief, and sometimes another, by some heavenly influence; ... men's spirits one while flourishing, another while barren, even as *fields are seen to be, what become of all those goodly prerogatives where-with we still flatter ourselves?" 155*

All this, of course, has a further bearing than Montaigne gives it in the context, and affects his own professed theology as it does the opinions he attacks; but none the less, the passage strikes at the dogmatists and the pragmatists of all the preceding schools, and hardily clears the ground 124 for a new inductive system. And in the last essay of all he makes a campaign against bad laws, which unsays many of his previous sayings on the blessedness of custom.

In tracing his influence elsewhere, it would be hard to point to an eminent French prose-writer who has not been affected by him. Sainte-Beuve finds 156 that La Bruy航 "at bottom is close to Montaigne, in respect not only of his style and his skilfully inconsequent method, but of his way of judging men and life"; and the literary heredity from Montaigne to Rousseau is recognised by all who have looked into the matter. The temperaments are profoundly different; yet the style of Montaigne had evidently taken as deep a hold of the artistic consciousness of Rousseau as had the doctrines of the later writers on whom he drew for his polemic. But indeed he found in the essay on the Cannibals the very theme of his first paradox; in Montaigne's emphatic denunciations 157 of laws more criminal than the crimes they dealt with, he had a deeper inspiration still; in the essay on the training 125 of children he had his starting-points for the argumentation of Emile; and in the whole unabashed self-portraiture of the Essays he had his great exemplar for the Confessions. Even in the very different case of Voltaire, we may go at least as far as Villemain and say that the essayist must have helped to shape the thought of the great freethinker; whose Philosophe Ignorant may indeed be connected with the Apology without any of the hesitation with which Villemain suggests his general parallel. In fine, Montaigne has scattered his pollen over all the literature of France. The most typical thought of La Rochefoucauld is thrown out 158 in the essay 159 De l'utile et de l'honneste; and the most modern-seeming currents of thought, as M. Stapfer remarks, can be detected in the passages of the all-discussing Gascon.

Among English-speaking writers, to say nothing of those who, like Sterne and Lamb, have been led by his example to a similar felicity of freedom in style, we may cite Emerson as one 126 whose whole work is coloured by Montaigne's influence, and Thoreau as one who, specially developing one side of Emerson's gospel, may be said to have found it all where Emerson found it, in the Essay on Solitude. 160 The whole doctrine of intellectual self-preservation, the ancient thesis "flee from the press and dwell in soothfastness," is there set forth in a series of ringing sentences, most of which, set in Emerson or Thoreau, would seem part of their text and thought. That this is no random attribution may be learned from the lecture on "Montaigne: the Sceptic," which Emerson has included in his Representative Men. "I remember," he says, telling how in his youth he stumbled on Cotton's translation, "I remember the delight and wonder in which I lived with it. It seemed to me as if I had myself written the book in some former life, so sincerely it spoke to my thought and experience." That is just what Montaigne has done for a multitude of others, in virtue of his prime quality of spontaneous self-expression. As Sainte-Beuve has it, there is a Montaigne in all of us. Flaubert, we know, read him constantly 127 for style; and no less constantly "found himself" in the self-revelation and analysis of the essays.

After all these testimonies to Montaigne's seminal virtue, and after what we have seen of the special dependence of Shakspere's genius on culture and circumstance, stimulus and initiative, for its evolution, there can no longer seem to an open mind anything of mere paradox in the opinion that the essays are the source of the greatest expansive movement of the poet's mind, the movement which made him — already a master of the whole range of passional emotion, of the comedy of mirth and the comedy and tragedy of sex — the great master of the tragedy of the moral intelligence. Taking the step from Julius Cæsar to Hamlet as corresponding to this movement in his mind, we may say that where the first play exhibits the concrete perception of the fatality of things, "the riddle of the painful earth"; in the second, in its final form, the perception has emerged in philosophic consciousness as a pure reflection. The poet has in the interim been revealed to himself; what he had perceived he now conceives. And 128 this is the secret of the whole transformation which the old play of Hamlet has received at his hands. Where he was formerly the magical sympathetic plate, receiving and rectifying and giving forth in inspired speech every impression, however distorted by previous instruments, that is brought within the scope of its action, he is now in addition the inward judge of it all, so much so that the secondary activity tends to overshadow the primary. The old Hamlet, it is clear, was a tragedy of blood, of physical horror. The least that Shakspere, at this age, could have done with it, would be to overlay and transform the physical with moral perception; and this has already been in part done in the First Quarto form. The mad Hamlet and the mad Ophelia, who had been at least as much comic as tragic figures in the older play, are already purified of that taint of their barbaric birth, save in so far as Hamlet still gibes at Polonius and jests with Ophelia in the primitive fashion of the pretended madman seeking his revenge. But the sense of the futility of the whole heathen plan, of the vanity of the revenge to which the Christian ghost hounds his son, of 129 the moral void left by the initial crime and its concomitants, not to be filled by any hecatomb of slain wrongdoers – the sense of all this, which is the essence of the tragedy, though so few critics seem to see it, clearly emerges only in the finished play. The dramatist is become the chorus to his plot, and the impression it all makes on his newly active spirit comes out in soliloquy after soliloquy, which hamper as much as they explain the action. In the old prose story, the astute barbarian takes a curiously circuitous course to his revenge, but at last attains it. In the intermediate tragedy of blood, the circuitous action had been preserved, and withal the revenge was attained only in the general catastrophe, by that daimonic "fortune" on which Montaigne so often enlarges. For Shakspere, then, with his mind newly at work in reverie and judgment, where before it had been but perceptive and reproductive, the theme was one of human impotence, failure of will, weariness of spirit in presence of over-mastering fate, recoil from the immeasurable evil of the world. Hamlet becomes the mouthpiece of the all-sympathetic spirit which has put itself in his place, 130 as it had done with a hundred suggested types before, but with a new inwardness of comprehension, a self-consciousness added to the myriad-sided consciousness of the past. Hence an involution rather than an elucidation of the play. There can be no doubt that Shakspere, in heightening and deepening the theme, has obscured it, making the scheming barbarian into a musing pessimist, who yet waywardly plays the mock-madman as of old, and kills the "rat" behind the arras; doubts the Ghost while acting on his message; philosophises with Montaigne and yet delays his revenge in the spirit of the Christianised savage, who fears to send the praying murderer to heaven. There is no solution of these anomalies: the very state of Shakspere's consciousness, working in his subjective way on the old material, made inevitable a moral anachronism and contradiction, analogous in its kind to the narrative anachronisms of his historical plays. But none the less, this tragedy, the first of the great group which above all his other work make him immortal, remains perpetually fascinating, by virtue even of that "pale cast of thought" which has "sicklied it 131 o'er" in the sense of making it too intellectual for dramatic unity and strict dramatic success. Between these undramatic, brooding soliloquies which stand so aloof from the action, but dominate the minds of those who read and meditate the text, and the old sensational elements of murder, ghost, fencing and killing, which hold the interest of the crowd — between these constituents, Hamlet remains the most familiar Shaksperean play.

This very pre-eminence and permanence, no doubt, will make many students still demur to the notion that a determining factor in the framing of the play was the poet's perusal of Montaigne's essays. And it would be easy to overstate that thesis in such a way as to make it untrue. Indeed, M. Chasles has, to my thinking, so overstated it. Had I come to his main proposition before realising the infusion of Montaigne's ideas in Hamlet, I think I should have felt it to be as excessive in the opposite direction as the proposition of Mr. Feis. Says M. Chasles: 161 —

132

"This date of 1603 (publication of Florio's translation) is instructive; the change in Shakspere's style dates from this very year. Before 1603, imitation of Petrarch, of Ariosto, and of Spenser is evident in his work: after 1603, this coquettish copying of Italy has disappeared; no more crossing rhymes, no more sonnets and concetti. All is reformed at once. Shakspere, who had hitherto studied the ancients only in the fashion of the fine writers of modern Italy, ... now seriously studies Plutarch and Sallust, and seeks of them those great teachings on human life with which the chapters of Michael Montaigne are filled. Is it not surprising to see Julius Cæsar and Coriolanus suddenly taken up by the man who has just (tout ·'heure) been describing in thirty-six stanzas, like Marini, the doves of the car of Venus? And does not one see that he comes fresh from the reading of Montaigne, who never ceased to translate, comment, and recommend the ancients...? The dates of Shakspere's Coriolanus, Cleopatra, and Julius Cæsar are incontestable. These dramas follow on from 1606 to 1608, with a rapidity which proves the fecund heat of an imagination still moved."

All this must be revised in the light of a more correct chronology. Shakspere's Julius Cæsar dates, not from 1604 but from 1600 or 1601, being referred to in Weever's Mirror of Martyrs, published in 1601, to say nothing of the reference in the third Act of Hamlet itself, where Polonius speaks of such a play. And, even if it had been written in 1604, it would still 133 *be a straining of the evidence to ascribe its production, with that of Coriolanus and Antony and Cleopatra, to the influence of Montaigne, when every one of these themes was sufficiently obtruded on the Elizabethan theatre by North's translation of Amyot's Plutarch. Any one who will compare Coriolanus with the translation in North will see that Shakspere has followed the text down to the most minute and supererogatory details, even to the making of blunders by putting the biographer's remarks in the mouths of the characters. The comparison throws a flood of light on Shakspere's mode of procedure; but it tells us nothing of his perusal of Montaigne. Rather it suggests a return from the method of the revised Hamlet, with its play of reverie, to the more strictly dramatic method of the chronicle histories, though with a new energy and concision of presentment. The real clue to Montaigne's influence on Shakspere beyond Hamlet, as we have seen, lies not in the Roman plays, but in Measure for Measure.*

There is a misconception involved, again, in M. Chasles' picture of an abrupt transition from 134 Shakspere's fantastic youthful method to that of Hamlet and the Roman plays. He overlooks the intermediate stages represented by such plays as Romeo and Juliet, Henry IV., King John, the Merchant of Venice, and As You Like It, all of which exhibit a great advance on the methods of Love's Labour Lost, with its rhymes and sonnets and "concetti." The leap suggested by M. Chasles is exorbitant; such a headlong development would be unintelligible. Shakspere had first to come practically into touch with the realities of life and character before he could receive from Montaigne the full stimulus he actually did undergo. Plastic as he was, he none the less underwent a normal evolution; and his early concreteness and verbalism and externality had to be gradually transmuted into a more inward knowledge of life and art before there could be superimposed on that the mood of the thinker, reflectively aware of the totality of what he had passed through.

Finally, the most remarkable aspect of Shakspere's mind is not that presented by Coriolanus and Antony and Cleopatra, which with 135 all their intense vitality represent rather his marvellous power of reproducing impressions than the play of his own criticism on the general problem of life. For the full revelation of this we must look rather in the great tragedies, notably in Lear, and thereafter in the subsiding movement of the later serious plays. There it is that we learn to give exactitude to our conception of the influence exerted upon him by Montaigne, and to see that, even as in the cases of Pascal and Montesquieu, Rousseau and Emerson, what happened was not a mere transference or imposition of opinions, but a living stimulus, a germination of fresh intellectual life, which developed under new forms. It would be strange if the most receptive and responsive of all the intelligences which Montaigne has touched should not have gone on differentiating itself from his.

VI.

136 What then is the general, and what the final relation of Shakspere's thought to that of Montaigne? How far did the younger man approve and assimilate the ideas of the elder, how far did he reject them, how far modify them? In some respects this is the most difficult part of our inquiry, were it only because Shakspere is firstly and lastly a dramatic writer. But he is not only that: he is at once the most subjective, the most sympathetic, and the most self-witholding of dramatic writers. Conceiving all situations, all epochs, in terms of his own psychology, he is yet the furthest removed from all dogmatic design on the opinions of his listeners; and it is only after a most vigilant process of moral logic that we can ever be justified in attributing to him this or that thesis of any one of his personages, apart from the general ethical sympathies which must be taken for granted. Much facile propaganda has been made by the device of crediting him in person with every religious 137 utterance found in his plays — even in the portions which analytical criticism proves to have come from other hands. Obviously we must look to his general handling of the themes with which the current religion deals, in order to surmise his attitude to that religion. And in the same way we must compare his general handling of tragic and moral issues, in order to gather his general attitude to the doctrine of Montaigne.

At the very outset, we must make a clean sweep of the strange proposition of Mr. Jacob Feis — that Shakspere deeply disliked the philosophy of Montaigne, and wrote Hamlet to discredit it. It is hard to realise how such a hopeless misconception can ever have arisen in the mind of anyone capable of making the historic research on which Mr. Feis seeks to found his assertion. If there were no other argument against it, the bare fact that the tragedy of Hamlet existed before Shakspere, and that he was, as usual, simply working over a play already on the boards, should serve to dismiss such a wild hypothesis. And from every other point of view, the notion is equally preposterous. 138

No human being in Shakspere's day could have gathered from Hamlet such a criticism of Montaigne as Mr. Feis reads into it by means of violences of interpretation which might almost startle Mr. Donnelly. Even if they blamed Hamlet for delaying his revenge, in the manner of the ordinary critical moralist, they could not possibly regard that delay as a kind of vice arising from the absorption of Montaignesque opinions. In the very year of the appearance of Florio's folio, it was a trifle too soon to make the assumption that Montaigne was demoralising mankind, even if we assume Shakspere to have ever been capable of such a judgment. And that assumption is just as impossible as the other. According to Mr. Feis, Shakspere detested such a creed and such conduct as Hamlet's, and made him die by poison in order to show his abhorrence of them — this, when we know Hamlet to have died by the poisoned foil in the earlier play. On that view, Cordelia died by hanging in order to show Shakspere's conviction that she was a malefactor; and Desdemona by stifling as a fitting punishment for adultery. The idea is outside of serious discus 139 sion. Barely to assume that Shakspere held Hamlet for a pitiable weakling is a sufficiently shallow interpretation of the play; but to assume that he made him die by way of condign punishment for his opinions is merely ridiculous. Once for all, there is absolutely nothing in Hamlet's creed or conduct which Shakspere was in a position to regard as open to his denunciation. The one intelligible idea which Mr. Feis can suggest as connecting Hamlet's conduct with Montaigne's philosophy is that Montaigne was a quietest, preaching and practising withdrawal from public broils. But Shakspere's own practice was on all fours with this. He sedulously held aloof from all meddling in public affairs; and as soon as he had gained a competence he retired, at the age of forty-seven, to Stratford-on-Avon. Mr. Feis's argument brings us to the very crudest form of the good old Christian verdict that if Hamlet had been a good and resolute man he would have killed his uncle out of hand, whether at prayers or anywhere else, and would then have married Ophelia, put his mother in a nunnery, and lived happily ever after. 162 And to that edifying 140 assumption, Mr. Feis adds the fantasy that Shakspere dreaded the influence of Montaigne as a deterrent from the retributive slaughter of guilty uncles by wronged nephews.

In the hands of Herr Stedefeld, who in 1871 anticipated Mr. Feis's view of Hamlet as a sermon against Montaigne, the thesis is not a whit more plausible. Herr Stedefeld entitles his book 163: "Hamlet: a Drama-with-a-purpose (Tendenzdrama) opposing the sceptical and cosmopolitan view of things taken by Michael de Montaigne"; and his general position is that Shakspere wrote the play as "the apotheosis of a practical Christianity," by way of showing how any one like Hamlet, lacking in Christian piety, and devoid of faith, love, and hope, must needs come to a bad end, even in a good cause. We are not entitled to charge Herr Stedefeld's thesis to the account of religious bias, seeing that Mr. Feis in his turn writes from the standpoint of a kind of Protestant freethinker, who sees in Shakspere a champion of free inquiry against the Catholic conformist policy of Montaigne; 141 while strictly orthodox Christians have found in Hamlet's various allusions to deity, and in his "as for me, I will go pray," a proof alike of his and of Shakspere's steadfast piety. Against all such superficialities of exegesis alike our safeguard must be a broad common-sense induction.

We are entitled to say at the outset, then, only this, that Shakspere at the time of working over Hamlet and Measure for Measure in 1603-1604 had in his mind a great deal of the reasoning in Montaigne's Essays; and that a number of the speeches in the two plays reproduce portions of what he had read. We are not entitled to assume that these portions are selected as being in agreement with Shakspere's own views: we are here limited to saying that he put certain of Montaigne's ideas or statements in the mouths of his characters where they would be appropriate. It does not follow that he shared the feelings of Claudio as to the possible life of the soul after death. And when Hamlet says to Horatio, on the strangeness of the scene with the Ghost:

> *"And therefore as a stranger give it welcome! 142 There are more things in heaven and earth, Horatio, Than are dreamt of in our philosophy" —*

though this may be said to be a summary of the whole drift of Montaigne's essay, 164 That it is folly to refer truth or falsehood to our sufficiency; and though we are entitled to believe that Shakspere had that essay or its thesis in his mind, there is no reason to suppose that the lines express Shakspere's own belief in ghosts. Montaigne had indicated his doubts on that head even in protesting against sundry denials of strange allegations: and it is dramatically fitting that Hamlet in the circumstances should say what he does. On the other hand, when the Duke in Measure for Measure, playing the part of a friar preparing a criminal for death, gives Claudio a consolation which does not contain a word of Christian doctrine, not a syllable of sacrificial salvation and sacramental forgiveness, we are entitled to infer from such a singular negative phenomenon, if not that Shakspere rejected the Christian theory of things, at least that it formed no part of his habitual thinking. It was the special business of the 143 Duke, playing in such a character, to speak to Claudio of sin and salvation, of forgiveness and absolution. Such a singular omission must at least imply disregard on the part of the dramatist. It is true that Isabella, pleading to Angelo in the second Act, speaks as a believing Christian on the point of forgiveness for sins; and the versification here is quite Shaksperean. But a solution of the anomaly is to be found here as elsewhere in the fact that Shakspere was working over an existing play; 165 and that in ordinary course he would, if need were, put the religious pleading of Isabella into his own magistral verse just as he would touch up the soliloquy of Hamlet on the question of killing his uncle at prayers — a soliloquy which we know to have existed in the earlier forms of the play. The writer who first made Isabella plead religiously with Angelo would have made the Duke counsel Claudio religiously. The Duke's speech, then, is to be regarded as Shakspere's special insertion; and it is to be taken as negatively exhibiting his opinions.

144

In the same way, the express withdrawal of the religious note at the close of Hamlet — where in the Second Quarto we have Shakspere making the dying prince say "the rest is silence" instead of "heaven receive my soul," as in the First Quarto — may reasonably be taken to express the same agnosticism on the subject of a future life as is implied in the Duke's speech to Claudio. It cannot reasonably be taken to suggest a purpose of holding Hamlet up to blame as an unbeliever, because Hamlet is made repeatedly to express himself, in talk and in soliloquy, as a believer in deity, in prayer, in hell, and in heaven. These speeches are mostly reproductions of the old play, the new matter being in the nature of the pagan allusion to the "divinity that shapes our ends." What is definitely Shaksperean is just the agnostic conclusion.

Did Shakspere, then, derive this agnosticism from Montaigne? What were really Montaigne's religious and philosophic opinions? We must consider this point also with more circumspection than has been shown by most of Montaigne's critics. The habit of calling him 145 "sceptic," a habit initiated by the Catholic priests who denounced his heathenish use of the term "Fortune," and strengthened by various writers from Pascal to Emerson, is a hindrance to an exact notion of the facts, inasmuch as the word "sceptic" has passed through two phases of significance, and may still have either. In the original sense of the term, Montaigne is a good deal of a "sceptic," because the main purport of the Apology of Raimond Sebonde appears to be the discrediting of human reason all round, and the consequent shaking of all certainty. And this method strikes not only indirectly but directly at the current religious beliefs; for Montaigne indicates a lack of belief in immortality, 166 besides repeatedly ignoring the common faith where he would naturally be expected to endorse it, as in the nineteenth and fortieth essays hereinbefore cited, and in his discussion of the Apology of Socrates. As is complained by Dean Church: 167 "His views, both of life and death, are absolutely and entirely un 146 affected by the fact of his profession to believe the Gospel." That profession, indeed, partakes rather obviously of the nature of his other formal salutes 168 to the Church, which are such as Descartes felt it prudent to make in a later generation. His profession of fidelity to Catholicism, again, is rather his way of showing that he saw no superiority of reasonableness in Protestantism, than the expression of any real conformity to Catholic ideals; for he indicates alike his aversion to heretic-hunting and his sense of the folly of insisting on the whole body of dogma. When fanatical Protestants, uncritical of their own creed, affected to doubt the sincerity of any man who held by Catholicism, he was naturally piqued. But he was more deeply piqued, as Naigeon has suggested, when the few but keen freethinkers of the time treated the Theologia Naturalis of Sebonde, which Montaigne had translated at his father's wish, as a feeble and inconclusive piece of argumentation; and it was primarily to retaliate on such critics — who on their part no doubt exhibited 147 some ill-founded convictions while attacking others — that he penned the Apology, which assails atheism in the familiar sophistical fashion, but with a most unfamiliar energy and splendour of style, as a manifestation of the foolish pride of a frail and perpetually erring reason. For himself, he was, as we have said, a classic theist, of the school of Cicero and Seneca; and as regards that side of his own thought he is not at all sceptical, save in so far as he nominally protested against all attempts to bring deity down to human conceptions, while himself doing that very thing, as every theist needs must.

Shakspere, then, could find in Montaigne the traditional deism of the pagan and Christian world, without any colour of specifically Christian faith, and with a direct lead to unbelief in a future state. But, whether we suppose Shakspere to have been already led, as he might be by the initiative of his colleague Marlowe, an avowed atheist, to agnostic views on immortality, or whether we suppose him to have had his first serious lead to such thought from Montaigne, we find him to all appearance carrying further the initial impetus, and proceeding 148 from the serene semi-Stoicism of the essayist to a deeper and sterner conception of things. It lay, indeed, in the nature of Shakspere's psychosis, so abnormally alive to all impressions, that when he fully faced the darker sides of universal drama, with his reflective powers at work, he must utter a pessimism commensurate with the theme. This is part, if not the whole, of the answer to the question "Why did Shakspere write tragedies?" 169 The whole answer can hardly be either Mr. Spedding's, that the poet wrote his darkest tragedies in a state of philosophic serenity, 170 or Dr. Furnivall's, that he "described hell because he had felt hell." 171 But when we find Shakspere writing a series of tragedies, including an extremely sombre comedy (Measure for Measure), after having produced mainly comedies and history-plays, we must conclude that the change was made of his own choice, and that whereas formerly his theatre took its comedies mostly from him, and its tragedies mostly from others, it now took its 149 comedies mostly from others and its tragedies from him. Further, we must assume that the gloomy cast of thought so pervadingly given to the new tragedies is partly a reflex of his own experience, but also in large part an expression of the philosophy to which he had been led by his reading, as well as by his life. For we must finally avow that the pervading thought in the tragedies outgoes the simple artistic needs of the case. In Othello we have indeed a very strictly dramatic array of the forces of wrong — weakness, blind passion, and pitiless egoism; but there is already a full suggestion of the overwhelming energy of the element of evil; and in Lear the conception is worked out with a desperate insistence which carries us far indeed from the sunny cynicism and prudent scepticism of Montaigne. Nowhere in the essays do we find such a note of gloom as is struck in the lines:

> *"As flies to wanton boys are we to the Gods: They kill us for their sport."*

And since there is no pretence of balancing that mordant saying with any decorous platitude of Christian Deism, we are led finally to the admission that Shakspere sounded a further depth 150 of philosophy than Montaigne's unembittered "cosmopolitan view of things." Instead of reacting against Montaigne's "scepticism," as Herr Stedefeld supposes, he produced yet other tragedies in which the wrongdoers and the wronged alike exhibit less and not more of Christian faith than Hamlet, 172 and in which there is no hint of any such faith on the part of the dramatist, but, on the contrary, a sombre persistence in the presentment of unrelieved evil. The utterly wicked Iago has as much of religion in his talk as anyone else in Othello, using the phrases "Christian and heathen," "God bless the mark," "Heaven is my judge," "You are one of those that will not serve God, if the devil bid you," "the little godliness I have," "God's will," and so forth; the utterly wicked Edmund in Lear, as we have seen, is made to echo Montaigne's "sceptical" passage on the subject of stellar influences, spoken with a moral purpose, rather than the quite contrary utterance in the Apology, in which the essayist, theistically bent on abasing human pretensions, gives to his scepticism the colour of a belief in those very 151 influences. 173 There is here, clearly, no pro-religious thesis. The whole drift of the play shows that Shakspere shares the disbelief in stellar control, though he puts the expression of the disbelief in the mouth of a villain; though he makes the honest Kent, on the other hand, declare that "it is the stars ... that govern our conditions;" 174 and though he had previously made Romeo speak of "the yoke of inauspicious stars," and the Duke describe mankind as "servile to all the skiey influences," and was later to make Prospero, in the Tempest 175 express his belief in "a most auspicious star." In the case of Montaigne, who goes on yet again to contradict himself in the Apology itself, satirising afresh the habit of associating deity with all human concerns, we are driven to surmise an actual variation of opinion — the vivacious intelligence springing this way or that according as it is reacting against the atheists or against the dogmatists. Montaigne, of course, is not a coherent philosopher; the way to systematic philosophic truth is a path too 152 steep to be climbed by such an undisciplined spirit as his, "sworn enemy to obligation, to assiduity, to constancy"; 176 and the net result of his "Apology" for Raimond Sebonde is to upset the system of that sober theologian as well as all others. Whether Shakspere, on the other hand, could or did detect all the inconsistencies of Montaigne's reasoning, is a point on which we are not entitled to more than a surmise; but we do find that on certain issues on which Montaigne dogmatises very much as did his predecessors, Shakspere applies a more penetrating logic, and explicitly reverses the essayist's verdicts. Montaigne, for instance, carried away by his master doctrine that we should live "according to nature," is given to talking of "art" and "nature" in the ordinary manner, carrying the primitive commonplace indeed to the length of a paradox. Thus in the essay on the Cannibals, 177 speaking of "savages," he protests that

"They are even savage, as we call those fruits wild which nature of herself and of her ordinary progress hath produced, whereas indeed they are those which ourselves have altered by our artificial devices, and diverted from their common order, we should rather 153 call savage. In those are the true and more profitable virtues and natural properties most lively and vigorous;" 178

deciding with Plato that

"all things are produced either by nature, by fortune, or by art; the greatest and fairest by one or other of the two first; the least and imperfect by this last."

And in the Apology, 179 after citing some as arguing that

"Nature by a maternal gentleness accompanies and guides" the lower animals, "as if by the hand, to all the actions and commodities of their life," while, "as for us, she abandons us to hazard and fortune, and to seek by art the things necessary to our conservation,"

though he proceeds to insist on the contrary that "nature has universally embraced all her creatures," man as well as the rest, and to argue that man is as much a creature of nature as the rest — since even speech, "if not natural, is necessary" — he never seems to come within sight of the solution that art, on his own showing, is just nature in a new phase. But to that point Shakspere proceeds at a stride in the Winter's Tale, one of the latest plays (? 1611), written about the time when we know him to 154 have been reading or re-reading the essay on the Cannibals. When Perdita refuses to plant gillyflowers in her garden,

> *"For I have heard it said There is an art which in their piedness shares With great creating nature,"*

the old king answers:

> *"Say there be: Yet nature is made better by no mean, But nature makes that mean; so o'er that art Which you say adds to nature, is an art That nature makes. You see, sweet maid, we marry A gentle scion to the wildest stock And make conceive a bark of baser kind By bud of nobler race: This is an art Which does mend nature — change it rather; but The art itself is nature." 180*

It is an analysis, a criticism, a philosophic demonstration; and the subtle poet smilingly lets us see immediately that he had tried the argument on the fanatics of "nature," fair or other, and knew them impervious to it. "I'll not put," says Puritan Perdita, after demurely granting that "so it is" —

155

"I'll not put The dibble in earth to set one slip of them."

The mind which could thus easily pierce below the inveterate fallacy of three thousand years of conventional speech may well be presumed capable of rounding Montaigne's philosophy wherever it collapses, and of setting it aside wherever it is arbitrary. Certain it is that we can never convict Shakspere of bad reasoning in person; and in his later plays we never seem to touch bottom in his thought. The poet of Venus and Adonis seems to have deepened beyond the plummet-reach even of the deep-striking intelligence that first stirred him to philosophise.

And yet, supposing this to be so, there is none the less a lasting community of thought between the two spirits, a lasting debt from the younger to the elder. Indeed, we cannot say that at all points Shakspere outwent his guide. It is a curious reflection that they had probably one foible in common; for we know Montaigne's little weakness of desiring his family to be thought ancient, of suppressing the fact of its recent establishment by commerce; and we have 156 evidence which seems to show that Shakspere sought zealously, 181 despite rebuffs, the formal constitution of a coat-of-arms for his family. On the other hand, there is nothing in Shakspere's work — the nature of the case indeed forbade it — to compare in democratic outspokenness with Montaigne's essay 182 Of the Inequality among us. The Frenchman's hardy saying 183 that "the souls of emperors and cobblers are all cast in one same mould" could not well be echoed in Elizabethan drama; and indeed we cannot well be sure that Shakspere would have endorsed it, with his fixed habit of taking kings and princes and generals and rich ones for his personages. But then, on the other hand, we cannot be sure that this was anything more than a part of his deliberate life's work of producing for the English multitude what that multitude cared to see, and catching London with that bait of royalty which commonly attracted it. It remains a fine question whether his extravagant idealisation and justification of Henry V. — which, though it 157 gives so little pause to some of our English critics, entitled M. Guizot to call him a mere John Bull in his ideas of international politics — it remains disputable whether this was exactly an expression of his own thought. It is notable that he never again strikes the note of blatant patriotism. And the poets of that time, further, seem to have had their tongues very much in their cheeks with regard to their Virgin Queen; so that we cannot be sure that Shakspere, paying her his fanciful compliment, 184 was any more sincere about it than Ben Jonson, who would do as much while privately accepting the grossest scandal concerning her. 185 It is certainly a remarkable fact that Shakspere abstained from joining in the poetic out-cry over her death, incurring reproof by his silence. 186

However all that may have been, we find Shakspere, after his period of pessimism, viewing life in a spirit which could be expressed in terms of Montaigne's philosophy. He certainly shaped his latter years in accordance with the 158 essayist's ideal. We can conceive of no other man in Shakspere's theatrical group deliberately turning his back, as he did, on the many-coloured London life when he had means to enjoy it at leisure, and seeking to possess his own soul in Stratford-on-Avon, in the circle of a family which had already lived so long without him. But that retirement, rounding with peace the career of manifold and intense experience, is a main fact in Shakspere's life, and one of our main clues to his innermost character. Emerson, never quite delivered from Puritan prepossessions, avowed his perplexity over the fact "that this man of men, he who gave to the science of mind a new and larger subject than had ever existed, and planted the standard of humanity some furlongs forward into Chaos — that he should not be wise for himself: it must even go into the world's history that the best poet led an obscure (!) and profane life, using his genius for the public amusement." If this were fundamentally so strange a thing, one might have supposed that the transcendentalist would therefore "as a stranger give it welcome." Approaching it on another plane, one finds 159 nothing specially perplexing in the matter. Shakspere's personality was an uncommon combination; but was not that what should have been looked for? And where, after all, is the evidence that he was "not wise for himself"? 187 Did he not make his fortune where most of his rivals failed? If he was "obscure," how otherwise could he have been less so? How could the bankrupt tradesman's son otherwise rise to fame? Should he have sought, at all costs, to become a lawyer, and rise perchance to the seat of Bacon, and the opportunity of eking out his stipend by bribes? If it be conceded that he must needs try literature, and such literature as a man could live by; and if it be further conceded that his plays, being so marvellous in their content, were well worth the writing, where enters the "profanity" of having written them, or of having acted in them, "for 160 the public amusement"? Even wise men seem to run special risks when they discourse on Shakspere: Emerson's essay has its own anomaly.

It is indeed fair to say that Shakspere must have drunk a bitter cup in his life as an actor. It is true that that calling is apt to be more humiliating than another to a man's self-respect, if his judgment remain sane and sensitive. We have the expression of it all in the Sonnets: 188

> *"Alas! 'tis true, I have gone here and there, And made myself a motley to the view, Gored mine own thoughts, sold cheap what is most dear, Made old offences of affections new."*

It is impossible to put into fewer and fuller words the story, many a year long, of sordid compulsion laid on an artistic nature to turn its own inner life into matter for the stage. But he who can read Shakspere might be expected to divine that it needed, among other things, even some such discipline as that to give his spirit its strange universality of outlook. And he who could esteem both Shakspere and Mon 161 taigne might have been expected to note how they drew together at that very point of the final retirement, the dramatic caterer finally winning, out of his earnings, the peace and self-possession that the essayist had inherited without toil. He must, one thinks, have repeated to himself Montaigne's very words 189: "My design is to pass quietly, and not laboriously, what remains to me of life; there is nothing for which I am minded to make a strain: not knowledge, of whatever great price it be." And when he at length took himself away to the quiet village of his birth, it could hardly be that he had not in mind those words of the essay 190 on Solitude:

"We should reserve a storehouse for ourselves ... altogether ours, and wholly free, wherein we may hoard up and establish our true liberty, the principal retreat and solitariness, wherein we must go alone to ourselves.... We have lived long enough for others, live we the remainder of all life unto ourselves.... Shake we off these violent hold-fasts which elsewhere engage us, and estrange us from ourselves. The greatest thing of the world is for a man to know how to be his own. It is high time to shake off society, since we can bring nothing to it...."

162

A kindred note is actually struck in the 146th Sonnet, 191 which tells of revolt at the expenditure of inner life on the outward garniture, and ex-horts the soul to live aright:

> *"Then soul live thou upon thy servant's loss, And let that live to aggravate thy store; Buy terms divine in selling hours of dross; Within be fed; without be rich no more: So shalt thou feed on death*

that feeds on men, And death once dead, there's no more dying then" —

an echo of much of Montaigne's discourse, herein before cited. 192

In perfect keeping with all this movement towards peace and contemplation, and in final keeping, too, with the deeper doctrine of Montaigne, is the musing philosophy which lights, as with a wondrous sunset, the play which one would fain believe the last of all. At the end, as at the beginning, we find the poet working on 163 a pre-existing basis, re-making an old play; and at the end, as at the beginning, we find him picturing, with an incomparable delicacy, new ideal types of womanhood, who stand out with a fugitive radiance from the surroundings of mere humanity; but over all alike, in the Tempest, there is the fusing spell of philosophic reverie. Years before, in Hamlet, he had dramatically caught the force of Montaigne's frequent thought that daylight life might be taken as a nightmare, and the dream life as the real. It was the kind of thought to recur to the dramatist above all men, even were it not pressed upon him by the essayist's reiterations:

"Those which have compared our life unto a dream, have happily had more reason so to do than they were aware. When we dream, our soul liveth, worketh, and exerciseth all her faculties, even and as much as when it waketh.... We wake sleeping, and sleep waking. In my sleep I see not so clear, yet can I never find my waking clear enough, or without dimness.... Why make we not a doubt whether our thinking and our working be another dreaming, and our waking some kind of sleeping?" 193

"Let me think of building castles in Spain, my imagination will forge me commodities and afford means 164 and delights wherewith my mind is really tickled and essentially gladded. How often do we pester our spirits with anger or sadness by such shadows, and entangle ourselves into fantastical passions which alter both our mind and body?... Enquire of yourself, where is the object of this alteration? Is there anything but us in nature, except subsisting nullity? over whom it hath any power?... Aristodemus, king of the Messenians, killed himself upon a conceit he took of some ill presage by I know not what howling of dogs.... It is the right way to prize one's life at the right worth of it, to forego it for a dream." 194

"... Our reasons do often anticipate the effect and have the extension of their jurisdiction so infinite, that they judge and exercise themselves in

inanity, and to a not being. Besides the flexibility of our invention, to frame reasons unto all manner of dreams; our imagination is likewise found easy to receive impressions from falsehood, by very frivolous appearances." 195

Again and again does the essayist return to this note of mysticism, so distinct from the daylight practicality of his normal utterance. And it was surely with these musings in his mind that the poet makes Prospero pronounce upon the phantasmagoria that the spirits have performed at his behest. We know, indeed, that the speech proceeds upon a reminiscence of four lines in the Earl of Stirling's Darius (1604), lines in them 165 selves very tolerable, alike in cadence and sonority, but destined to be remembered by reason of the way in which the master, casting them into his all-transmuting alembic, has remade them in the fine gold of his subtler measure. The Earl's lines run:

> *"Let greatness of her glassy scepters vaunt; Not scepters, no, but reeds, soon bruised, soon broken; And let this worldly pomp our wits enchant; All fades, and scarcely leaves behind a token. Those golden palaces, those gorgeous halls, With furniture superfluously fair; Those stately courts, those sky-encountering walls, Evanish all like vapours in the air."*

The sonorities of the rhymed verse seem to have vibrated in the poet's brain amid the memories of the prose which had suggested to him so much; and the verse and prose alike are raised to an immortal movement in the great lines of Prospero:

> *"These our actors, As I foretold you, are all spirits, and Are melted into air, into thin air. And like the baseless fabric of this vision, The cloud-capped towers, the gorgeous palaces, The solemn temples, the great globe itself, Yea, all which it inherits, shall dissolve 166 And, like this unsubstantial pageant faded, Leave not a wrack behind. We are such stuff As dreams are made on, and our little life Is rounded with a sleep."*

In the face of that vast philosophy, it seems an irrelevance to reason, as some do, that in the earlier scene in which Gonzalo expounds his Utopia of incivilisation, Shakspere so arranges the dialogue as to express his own ridicule of the conception. The interlocutors, it will be remembered, are Sebastian and Antonio, two of the villains of the piece, and Alonso, the wrecked usurper. The kind Gonzalo talks of the ideal community to distract Alonso's troubled thoughts; Sebastian and Antonio jeer at him; and Alonso finally cries, "Pr'ythee, no more, thou dost talk nothing to me." Herr Gervinus is quite sure that this was meant to state Shakspere's prophetic derision for all communisms and socialisms and peace congresses, Shakspere being the fore-ordained oracle of the political gospel of his German commentators, on the principle of "Gott mit uns." And it may well have been that Shakspere, looking on the society of his age, had no faith in any Utopia, and that he humorously put what 167 he felt to be a valid criticism of Montaigne's in the mouth of a surly rascal — he has done as much elsewhere. But he was surely the last man to have missed seeing that Montaigne's Utopia was no more Montaigne's personal political counsel to his age than As You Like It was his own; and, as regards the main purpose of Montaigne's essay, which was to show that civilisation was no unmixed gain as contrasted with some forms of barbarism, the author of Cymbeline was hardly the man to repugn it, even if he amused himself by putting forward Caliban 196 as the real "cannibal," in contrast to Montaigne's. He had given his impression of certain aspects of civilisation in Hamlet, Measure for Measure, and King Lear. As his closing plays show, however, he had reached the knowledge that for the general as for the private wrong, the sane man must cease to cherish indignation. That teaching, which he could not didactically impose, for such a world as his, on the old tragedy of revenge which he recoloured with Montaigne's thought, he found didactically enough set down in the essay on Diversion: 197

168

"Revenge is a sweet pleasing passion, of a great and natural impression: I perceive it well, albeit I have made no trial of it. To divert of late a young prince from it, I told him not he was to offer the one side of his cheek to him who had struck him on the other in regard of charity; nor displayed I unto him the tragical events poesy bestoweth upon that passion. There I left him and strove to make him taste the beauty of a contrary image; the honour, the favour, and the goodwill he should acquire by gentleness and goodness; I diverted him to ambition."

And now it is didactically uttered by the wronged magician in the drama: —

*"Though with their high wrongs I am struck to the quick, Yet with
my nobler reason, 'gainst my fury Do I take part; the rarer action
is In virtue than in vengeance...."*

*The principle now pervades the whole of Prospero's society; even the
cursed and cursing Caliban is recognised 198 as a necessary member of
it: —*

*"We cannot miss him; he does make our fire, Fetch in our wood;
and serves in offices That profit us."*

*It is surely not unwarrantable to pronounce, then, finally, that the poet
who thus watchfully lit his action from the two sides of passion and 169
sympathy was in the end at one with his "guide, philosopher, and friend,"
who in that time of universal strife and separateness could of his own ac-
cord renew the spirit of Socrates, and say: 199 "I esteem all men my com-
patriots, and embrace a Pole even as a Frenchman, subordinating this
national tie to the common and universal." Here, too, was not Montaigne
the first of the moderns?*

*1 Preface to Eng. trans. of Simrock on The Plots of Shakespere's Plays,
1850.*

2
*Lady Politick Would-be: All our English writers, I mean such as are happy
in the Italian, Will deign to steal out of this author [Pastor Fido] mainly
Almost as much as from Montaignie; He has so modern and facile a vein,
— Act iii. sc. 2.*

3 London and Westminster Review, July, 1838, p. 321.

*4 Article in Journal des D颖ts, 7 November, 1846, reprinted in
L'Angleterre au Seizi警 Si裱e, ed. 1879, p. 136.*

5 Montaigne (S鲩e des Grands Ecrivains Fran哲s), 1895, p. 105.

6 Moli肮 et Shakspere.

7 Shakspere and Classical Antiquity, Eng. tr. p. 297.

*8 See this point discussed in the Free Review of July, 1895: and compare
the lately published essay of Mr. John Corbin, on The Elizabethan Hamlet,
(Elkin Matthews, 1895).*

9 *Hamlet, Act V, scene 2.*

10 *Book I, Essay 33.*

11 *Advice in Florio.*

12 *B. III, Ch. 8. Of the art of conferring.*

13 *B. III, Ch. 12.*

14 *Act II, Sc. 1, 144.*

15 *Book I, ch. II, end.*

16 *Book I, ch. 23.*

17 *Ibid.*

18 *Some slip of the pen seems to have occurred in this confused line. The original Et male consultis pretium est: prudentia fallax — is sufficiently close to Shakspere's phrase.*

19 *"O heaven! a beast that wants discourse of reason" (Act I, Scene 2.)*

20 *Act II, Sc. 2.*

21 *Act IV, Scene 2.*

22 *Act IV, Scene 4.*

23 *See Furniss's Variorum edition of Hamlet, in loc.*

24 *B. I. Chap. 19; Edit. Firmin-Didot, vol. i, p. 68.*

25 *B. II, Chap. 4; Ed. cited, p. 382.*

26 *B. II. Chap. 12; Ibid, p. 459.*

27 *B. II. Chap. 33.*

28 *Shakespere and Montaigne, 1884, p. 88.*

29 *B. III, Chap. 12.*

30 *Act III, Scene 3.*

31 *B. I, ch. 22.*

32 *Act II, Scene 2.*

33 *Othello, Act II, Scene 3.*

34 *B. I, ch. 40, "That the taste of goods or evils doth greatly depend on the opinion we have of them."*

35 B. I, ch. 50.

36 B. I, ch. 22.

37 B. III, ch. 10.

38 Act V, Scene 4.

39 On reverting to Mr. Feis's book I find that in 1884 he had noted this and others of the above parallels, which I had not observed when writing on the subject in 1883. In view of some other parallels and clues drawn by him, our agreements leave me a little uneasy. He decides, for instance (p. 93) that Hamlet's phrase "foul as Vulcan's stithy" is a "sly thrust at Florio" who in his preface calls himself "Montaigne's Vulcan"; that the Queen's phrase "thunders in the index" is a reference to "the Index of the Holy See and its thunders"; and that Hamlet's lines "Why let the stricken deer go weep" are clearly a satire against Montaigne, "who fights shy of action." Mr. Feis's book contains so many propositions of this order that it is difficult to feel sure that he is ever judicious. Still, I find myself in agreement with him on some four or five points of textual coincidence in the two authors.

40 Act I, Scene 4.

41 B. II, Chap. 33.

42 It is further relevant to note that in the essay Of Drunkenness (ii. 2) Montaigne observes that "drunkenness amongst others appeareth to me a gross and brutish vice," that "the worst estate of man is where he loseth the knowledge and government of himself," and that "the grossest and rudest nation that liveth amongst us at this day, is only that which keepeth it in credit." The reference is to Germany: but Shakspere in Othello (Act II, Sc. 3) makes Iago pronounce the English harder drinkers than either the Danes or the Hollanders; and the lines:

"This heavy-headed revel, east and west, Makes us traduced and taxed of other nations; They clepe us drunkards, and with swinish phrase, Soil our addition."

might also be reminiscent of Montaigne, though of course there is nothing peculiar in such a coincidence.

43 B. III, Chap. 7.

44 B. III, Chap. 4.

45 B. III, Chap. 10.

46 B. III, Chap. 2.

47 B. III, Chap. 13.

48 B. I, Chap. 38.

49 B. III, Chap. 4.

50 B. I, Chap. 40.

51 B. II, Chap. 8.

52 B. II, Chap. 18.

53 De Officus i, 4: cf. 30.

54 1534, 1558, 1583, 1600. See also the compilation entitled *A Treatise of Morall Philosophie* by W. Baudwin, 4th enlargement by T. Paulfreyman. 1600, pp. 44-46, where there is a closely parallel passage from Zeno as well as that of Cicero.

55 Mr. Feis makes this attribution.

56 B. II, Chap. 1.

57 This may fairly be argued, perhaps, even of the somewhat close parallel, noted by Mr. Feis, between Laertes' lines (I, 3):

"For nature, crescent, does not grow alone In thews and bulk, but as this temple waxes The inward service of the mind and soul Grows wide withal,"

and Florio's rendering of an extract from Lucretius in the Apology

"The mind is with the body bred, we do behold. It jointly grows with it, it waxeth old."

Only the slight coincidence of the use of the (then familiar) verb "wax" in both passages could suggest imitation in the case of such a well-worn commonplace.

58 See some cited at the close of this essay in another connection.

59 B. II, Chap. 12.

60 Act IV, Scene 3.

61 "Le monde est un branloire perenne" (Book III, Essay 2). Florio translates that particular sentence: "The world runs all on wheels" a bad rendering.

62 B. III, Chap. 3.

63 B. II, Chap. 17.

64 It may fairly be laid down as practically certain, from what we know of the habit of circulating works in manuscript at that period, and from what Florio tells us in his preface, that translations of some of the essays had been passed about before Florio's folio was printed.

65 Varia Historia, XII, 23.

66 The story certainly had a wide vogue, being found in Aristotle, Eudemian Ethics, iii, 1, and in Nicolas of Damascus; while Strabo (vii, ii. 1) gives it further currency by contradicting it as regards the Cimbri.

67 B. II, Chap. 5.

68 B. II, Chap. 3.

69 Richard III, I, 4; V, 3.

70 The Influence of Seneca on Elizabethan Tragedy, 1893, p. 80-5.

71 Actus III, 865-866.

72 Actus IV, 1526-7.

73 This in turn is an echo from the Greek. See note in Doering's edition.

74 See Boswell's edition of Malone's Shakspere, in loc.

75 Yet again, in Marston's Insatiate Countess, the commentators have noticed the same sentiment.

"Death, From whose stern cave none tracks a backward path."

It was in fact a poetic commonplace.

76 Act 5, Scene 6.

77 Act v, sc. 1.

78 I, 22.

79 2 H. IV., iv. 3

80 ii. 2

81 ii. 10.

82 So far as I remember, the idea of suicide as a desertion of one's post without the deity's permission is first found, in English literature, in Sidney, and he would find it in Montaigne's essay on the Custom of the Isle of Cea (edit. Firmin-Didot, i, 367).

83 When this is compared with the shorter speech of similar drift in the anonymous play of Edward III. ("To die is all as common as to live" etc., Act iv., sc. 4) it will be seen that the querying form as well as the elaboration constitutes a special resemblance between the speech in Shakspere and the passages in Montaigne

84 Apology of Raimond Sebonde.

85 ii, 6, Of Exercise or Practice.

86 Apology.

87 Ibid., near end.

88 On Isis and Osiris, c. 26.

89 Canto v.

90 Canto xxxii.

91 It would seem to be from those early monkish legends that the medi漀l Inferno was built up. The torture of cold was the northern contribution to the scheme. Compare Warton, History of English Poetry, sec. 49, and Wright's Saint Patrick's Purgatory, 1844, p. 18.

92 Paradise Lost, B. II., 587-603.

93 Edit. Firmin-Didot. i, 597-598.

94 Ibid. p. 621.

95 Act iv., sc. 5.

96 iii. 3.

97 B. v, cc. 8, 9, 10. Cf. vi. 2, 3.

98 B. v, cc. 22-25.

99 ii. 32.

100 The arguments of Dr. Karl Elze, in his Essays on Shakspere (Eng. tr., p. 15), to show that the Tempest was written about 1604, seem to me to possess no weight whatever. He goes so far as to assume that the speech of Prospero in which Shakspere transmutes four lines of the Earl of Stirling's Darius must have been written immediately after the publication of that work. The argument is (1) that Shakspere must have seen Darius when it came out, and (2) that he would imitate the passage then or never.

101 Act v, sc. 3.

102 i, 31.

103 ii, 13.

104 Act i, sc. 2.

105 Act iv. sc. 3.

106 i, 2.

107 Hippolytus, 615 (607).

108 See the Prologue to Every Man in His Humour, first ed., preserved by Gifford.

109 The 29th.

110 See his Characteristics of English Poets, 2nd. ed. p. 222.

111 The most elaborate and energetic attempt to prove Shakspere classically learned is that made in the Critital Observations on Shakspere (1746) of the Rev. John Upton, a man of great erudition and much random acuteness (shown particularly in bold attempts to excise interpolations from the Gospels), but as devoid of the higher critical wisdom as was Bentley, whom he congenially criticised. To a reader of to-day, his arguments from Shakspere's diction and syntax are peculiarly unconvincing.

112 It may not be out of place here to say a word for Farmer in passing, as against the strictures of M. Stapfer, who, after recognising the general pertinence of his remarks, proceeds to say (Shakspere and Classical Antiquity, Eng. trans, p. 83) that Farmer "fell into the egregious folly of speaking in a strain of impertinent conceit: it is as if the little man for little he must assuredly have been – was eaten up with vanity." This is in its way as unjust as the abuse of Knight. M. Stapfer has misunderstood Farmer's tone, which is one of banter against, not Shakspere, but those critics who blunderingly ascribed to him a wide and close knowledge of the classics. Towards Shakspere, Farmer was admiringly appreciative – and in the preface to the second edition of his essay he wrote: "Shakspere wanted not the stilts of languages to raise him above all other men."

113 Ch. iv. of vol. cited.

114 The Influence of Seneca on Elizabethan Tragedy, pp. 66-67.

115 Hercules Furens, ad fin. (1324-1329.).

116 Hippolytus, Act. II, 715-718 (723-726.)

117 Choephori, 63-65.

118 Carm. lxxxviii, In Gellium. See the note in Dœring's edition.

119 Gerusalemme, xviii, 8.

120 The Insatiate Countess, published in 1613.

121 Hamlet, Act iv. sc. 3.

122 Agamemnon, 152-153.

123 ii, 3 (near beginning.)

124 Hercules Furens, Act. V. 1261-2.

125 Act iv, Sc. 3.

126 Hercules Furens, 1258-61.

127 Macbeth, Act v, Sc. 2.

128 Ibid. Act iv, Sc. 2.

129 Ibid. Act i, sc. 7.

130 B. ii. ch. 10.

131 Tschischwitz, Shakspere-Forschungen, i, 1868, S. 52.

132 "Es ist ubrigens nicht zu bedauern dass Shakspere Brunos Komodie nicht durchweg zum Muster genommen, den sie enthält so masslose Obscönitäten, dass Shakspere an seinen stärksten Stellen daneben fast jungfräulich erscheint" (Work cited, S. 52).

133 Work cited, S. 57. I follow Dr. Tschischwitz's translation, so far as syntax permits.

134 Act i, Sc. 4.

135 Work cited, Sc. 59.

136 See Frith's Life of Giordano Bruno, 1889, pp. 121-128.

137 Act v, Sc. 1.

138 Cited by Noack, art. Bruno, in Philosophie-geschichtliches Lexikon.

139 Act i, Sc. 2.

140 Work cited, p. 90.

141 It would be unjust to omit to acknowledge that Dr. Furnivall seeks to frame an inductive notion of Shakspere, even when rejecting good evidence and proceeding on deductive lines; that in the works of Professor

Dowden on Shakspere there is always an effort towards a judicial method, though he refuses to take some of the most necessary steps; and that the work of Mr. Appleton Morgan, President of the New York Shakspere Society, entitled Shakspere in Fact and Criticism (New York, 1888), is certainly not open to the criticism I have passed. Mr. Morgan's essentially rationalistic attitude is indicated in a sentence of his preface: "My own idea has been that William Shakspere was a man of like passions with ourselves, whose moods and veins were influenced, just as are ours, by his surroundings, employments, vocations ... and that, great as he was, and oceanic as was his genius, we can read him all the better because he was, after all, a man...." In recognising the good sense of Mr. Morgan's general attitude, I must not be understood to endorse his rejection of the "metrical tests" of Mr. Fleay and other English critics. These seem to me to be about the most important English contribution to the scientific comprehension of Shakspere. On the other hand, it may be said that the naturalistic conception of Shakspere as an organism in an environment was first closely approached in the present century by French critics, as Guizot and Chasles (Taine's picture of the Elizabethan theatre, adopted by Green, having been founded on a study by Chasles); that the naturalistic comprehension of Hamlet, as an incoherent whole resulting from the putting of new cloth into an old garment, was first reached by the German Rmelin (Shakspere Studien); and that the structural anomalies of Hamlet as an acting play were first clearly put by the German Benedix (Die Shakspereomanie) these two critics thus making amends for much vain discussion of Hamlet by their countrymen before and since; while the naturalistic conception of the man Shakspere is being best developed at present in America. The admirable work of Messrs. Clarke and Wright and Fleay in the analysis of the text and the revelation of its non-Shaksperean elements, seems to make little impression on English culture; while such a luminous manual as Mr. Barrett Wendell's William Shakspere: a Study in Elizabethan Literature (New York, 1894), with its freshness of outlook and appreciation, points to decided progress in rational Shakspere-study in the States, though, like the Shakspere Primer of Professor Dowden, it is not consistently scientific throughout.

142 Life of Shakspere, 1886, p. 128.

143 See Mr. Appleton Morgan's Shakspere's Venus and Adonis: a Study in Warwickshire Dialect.

144 Professor Dowden notes in his Shakspere Primer (p. 12) that before 1600 the prices paid for plays, by Henslowe, the theatrical lessee, vary from

4 to 8, and not till later did it rise as high as 20 for a play by a popular dramatist.

145

Compare the 78th Sonnet, which ends; —

But thou art all my art, and dost advance As high as learning my rude ignorance.

146 Life of Shakspere, pp. 29, 128.

147 See it in his Life of Shakspere, pp. 120-124. Mr. Fleay's theory, though perhaps the best "documented" of all, has received little attention in comparison with Mr. Tyler's, which has the attraction of fuller detail.

148 Only in Chaucer (e.g., The Book of the Duchess) do we find before his time the successful expression of the same perception; and Chaucer counted for almost nothing in Elizabethan letters.

149 See Fleay's Life of Shakspere, pp. 130-1.

150 Cp. the Essays, ii, 17: iii, 2. (Edit. cited, vol. ii, pp. 40, 231.)

151 Essays, i, 25; cf. i, 48. (Edit. cited, vol. i, pp. 304, 429.)

152 ii, 4. (Edit. cited, i, 380.)

153 ii, 10. (Edit. cited, i, 429.)

154 Pens饼 Diverses. Less satisfying is the further pens饼/i> in the same collection: — "Les quatre grand po봉s, Platon, Malebranche, Shaftes-bury, Montaigne."

155 Edition cited, i, 622-623.

156 Port Royal, 4i警 餘t., ii. 400, note.

157 B. iii, Chap. 13.

158 "In the midst of our compassion, we feel within I know not what bitter sweet touch of malign pleasure in seeing others suffer." (Comp. La Rochefoucauld, Pens饼/i> 104.)

159 B. iii, Chap. 1.

160 i, Chap. 38.

161 L'Angleterre au Seizi警 Si褄e, p. 133.

162 This seems to be the ideal implied in the criticisms even of Mr. Lowell and Mr. Dowden.

163 Hamlet: ein Tendenzdrama Sheakspere's [sic throughout book] gegen die skeptische und cosmopolitische Weltanschanung des Michael de Montaigne, von G. F. Stedefeld, Kreisgerichtsrath, Berlin. 1871.

164 B. i, Chap. 26.

165 It is not disputed that the plot existed beforehand in Whetstone's Promos and Cassandra; and there was probably an intermediate drama.

166 Edit. Firmin-Didot, i, 590.

167 Oxford Essays, p. 279. Sterling, from his Christian-Carlylese point of view, declared of Montaigne that "All that we find in him of Christianity would be suitable to apes and dogs rather than to rational and moral beings" (London and Westminster Review, July, 1838, p. 340.)

168 Sainte-Beuve has noted how in the essay on Prayer he added many safeguarding clauses in the later editions.

169 See Mr. Spedding's essay, so entitled, in the Cornhill Magazine, August, 1880.

170 Art. cited, end.

171 Note cited by Mr. Spedding. Cp. Introd. to Leopold Shakspere p. lxxxvii.

172 Lear once (iii. 4) says he will pray; but his religion goes no further.

173 See the passage cited above in section iii in connection with Measure for Measure.

174 Act iv., Sc. 2.

175 Act i, Sc. 2.

176 B. i, Chap. 20.

177 B. i, Chap. 30.

178 Edit. Firmin-Didot, i, 202.

179 Ibid., pp. 477-478.

180 Here, it may be said, there is a trace of the influence of Bruno's philosophy; and it may well be that Shakspere did not spontaneously strike out the thought for himself. But I am not aware that any parallel passage has been cited.

181 Fleay's Life, pp. 138, &c.

182 B. i, Chap. 42.

183 B. ii, Chap. 12. (Edit. cited, i, 501.)

184 Midsummer Nights Dream, Act ii. Sc. 2.

185 See his Conversations with Drummond of Hawthornden

186 Halliwell-Phillipps, Outlines of the Life of Shakspere, 5th ed., p. 175.

187 I find even Mr. Appleton Morgan creating a needless difficulty on this head. In his Shakspere in Fact and Criticism, already cited, he writes (p. 316): "I find him ... living and dying so utterly unsuspicious that he had done anything of which his children might care to hear, that he never even troubled himself to preserve the manuscript of or the literary property in a single one of the plays which had raised him to affluence." As I have already pointed out, there is no reason to suppose that Shakspere could retain the ownership of his plays any more than did the other writers who supplied his theatre. They belonged to the partnership. Besides, he could not possibly have published as his the existing mass, so largely made up of other men's work. His fellow-players did so without scruple after his death, being simply bent on making money.

188 Sonnet 110. Compare the next.

189 B. ii, Chap. 10.

190 B. i, Chap. 38.

191 This may be presumed to have been written between 1603 and 1609, the date of the publication of the Sonnets. As Mr. Minto argues, "the only sonnet of really indisputable date is the 107th, containing the reference to the death of Elizabeth" (Characteristics, as cited, p. 220). As the first 126 sonnets make a series, it is reasonable to take those remaining as of later date.

192 It more particularly echoes, however, two passages in the nineteenth essay: "There is no evil in life for him that hath well conceived, how the privation of life is no evil. To know how to die, doth free us from all subjection and constraint." "No man did ever prepare himself to quit the world more simply and fully ... than I am fully assured I shall do. The deadest deaths are the best"

193 ii, 12.

194 iii, 11.

195 iii, 4.

196 In all probability this character existed in the previous play, the name being originally, as was suggested last century by Dr. Farmer, a mere variant of "Canibal."

197 iii, 4.

198 Act ii, Sc. 2.

199 iii, 9.

170

BY THE SAME AUTHOR.

BUCKLE AND HIS CRITICS: A Study in Sociology.

THE SAXON AND THE CELT: A Study in Sociology.

ESSAYS TOWARDS A CRITICAL METHOD: New Series.

MODERN HUMANISTS.

THE FALLACY OF SAVING: A Study in Economics.

THE EIGHT HOURS QUESTION: A Study in Economics.

CHRIST AND KRISHNA: A Study in Mythology. Etc. Etc.

THE UNIVERSITY PRESS, LIMITED,

16, John Street, Bedford Row, London, W.C.

Now Ready 2s. 6d. net.

THE BLIGHT OF RESPECTABILITY.

An Anatomy of the Disease and a Theory of Curative Treatment.

By Geoffrey Mortimer.

THE SAXON AND THE CELT.

By John M. Robertson.

PRESS OPINIONS.

Daily Chronicle:

Although the title of this book defines its scope, it does not indicate its main purpose. That is to show that the Celtic race has been misrepresented by a number of historians, from Mommsen to Froude, as incapable of self-government; and to prove, by inference, its fitness for Home Rule.... The major argument is based by Mommsen and his school on the assumption of permanent distinctions among races; and therefore Mr. Robertson applies himself, with a large measure of success, to the task of showing that the theory of innate persistent qualities marking off one people from another has no ethnological justification.... Mr. Robertson is able to make short and easy work of the loose writing which sums up those (imaginary) characters in epithet or epigram.... Mr. Robertson's lively style and happy allusiveness keep the reader interested to the end...

Just published, 10s. net,

PSEUDO-PHILOSOPHY

AT THE END OF THE NINETEENTH CENTURY.

By Hugh Mortimer Cecil.

PRESS OPINIONS.

The Sun, March 31, 1897:

The author of "Pseudo-Philosophy" handles his weapons well, and seems to us in many instances to occupy positions which, with our present human intelligence, are almost unassailable. On the other hand, of course, champions of orthodoxy, as a rule, frankly admit that some of their tenets and the justice of certain aspects of the divine policy cannot be comprehended by the natural man. But Mr. Cecil's strong feelings occasionally carry him too far, as when in the preface he seems to use "religious obscurantism" as a synonym for religion generally. The former may have been opposed to social progress, as he says. To contend that the same charge will stand against the latter is only to ignore the fact, if not indeed the law, that the great social awakenings have almost invariably followed hard upon the great religious revivals.